AT NIGHT ONLY

CHRISTOPHER STODDARD

ITNA PRESS
Los Angeles, CA
www.itnapress.com

This is a work of fiction. Names, characters, places, and incidents are a product of the author's imagination. Locales and public names are sometimes used for atmospheric purposes. Any resemblance to actual people, living or dead, or to businesses, companies, events, institutions, or locales is completely coincidental.

Cover design and photo courtesy of Christopher Stoddard Copyright © 2023

Christopher Stoddard. – 1st ed.
ISBN 978-0-9976432-1-3

PART I

MOURNING

For G in the Lake of Fire

When you are dead to the world,
the world often rescues you,
if only to make a figure of fun out of you.

—Jean Rhys, *Good Morning Midnight*

THIS IS FOREST: a gated lot on Kent Avenue stocked with luxury patio furniture, green plants, baby trees and bright flowers price-tagged for the terribly obvious, oblivious residents of Williamsburg. A big old weeping willow stands at its entrance, a remnant of a neighborhood ghosted for years before the money moved in. That's the tool shed where Shoshanna and I one night last summer filled our bodies with tools of intoxication, confessed our dark pasts, showed off the faded scars on our arms, the keloids on our minds. And over there on the glass-and-gunmetal console where the iPad cash register sits is a poster-size photo collage of her, chronicling her infancy to the presently past day of a lively girl of twenty-nine: virtually clear eyes with just a hint of blue, round face, thin lips and straight blond hair—she'd have been prettier if she were thinner, but the booze paid its toll in body fat. There's a smaller collage on a dainty patio table. The images of her are making tears fall from the eyes of those staring at them: family, friends, party buddies like me. I suppose it's only fitting that her memorial is at her place of employment, considering how much time she spent here.

Shoshanna and I were little more than acquaintances, but when I'm expressing my condolences to the father—"She was a great girl"—the palpability of his grief as he's shaking my hand is somehow infecting my nervous system, making me cry. I feel like an imposter because I'm never truly sad when someone I know dies. I guess I must have some compassion after all, just enough to remain human.

Everyone's getting drunk rather quickly, which I find a bit ironic since the drink is what fueled Shoshanna's demise. I doubt she'd have fallen from the roof of that brownstone up the street had she not have been so wasted. Then again, there are rumors of her abusive boyfriend tossing her over. One way or another she's dead.

More than anything, as I stand here absorbing the scene, I'm feeling a bit jealous. She took the brave way out. Murderous boyfriend who beats or booze-poisoned blood—either or both were bold moves I wish I'd thought of first. Stewing secretly, I'm teetering between a smile and a sad face like a comedy-slash-tragedy mask, resisting the occasional wave of grief infecting my otherwise numb self, all the while daydreaming of my own body rotting.

I spot Shoshanna's boyfriend peering through the gated entrance to the garden, the shed, her memorial service, his eyes seeming to hollow out as the shadow of the posh apartment complex behind the lot grows in the quickly receding daylight. My former best friend Pedro and his girlfriend Nico—real friends of hers—are sitting across the lot in a larger version of the tool shed that's used as an office. Pedro is sobbing on Nico's shoulder. With a couple nods, I get their attention, my eyes then gesturing toward the gate.

I'd found it strange Pedro needed to tell me about Shoshanna's death after not communicating with me for as long as he had. Binge-watching in bed some awful Hulu Original Series, I received his text to call him right away—he had some news to share. Instead of hello: "Shoshanna died. I thought you'd want to know." Never considered her a good friend. In retrospect, I *had* known her for years, having spent many a moon on molly in passionate conversation with her. Other than Pedro, she was the only one to whom I ever divulged the horrors of my past. Something about her energy compelled me to tell her everything. Perhaps I intuited her death and the fact that my sad tales would be buried with her.

Pedro and Nico walk sullenly toward the makeshift bar I've been generously tending for the last half-hour or so—my limited knowledge of mixing alcohol a non-issue because the only drinks on the menu are beer from a keg, screw-capped wine and bottled water. My shift is up, the next one having been assigned to Amanda, Shoshanna's former roommate, an emaciated white chick from Florida who claims to have been her best friend; but I've seen her creeping out of the boyfriend's pickup truck at a garden party or two. Heard she ransacked Shoshanna's room for jewelry under the guise of wanting "something to remember her by."

"Someone should tell him to get out of here before her father sees him," I say.

Pedro's eyes are red like the beach ball in those old Visine commercials, and for once it's not from drugs and lack of sleep.

I've only seen him cry one other time—when Nico was threatening to leave him—and I've known him for four years.

"It doesn't matter. He can't get in here," he says dully.

Nico grips his shoulder, keeping him steady in his grief.

"I'll take it from here, sugar," says Amanda. "Fuck, I need a drink! This memorial is depressing the shit out of me."

"All yours," I grumble. There may be a handsome blonde hiding behind the cracked-out stick before me, but I doubt she'll ever be realized. Met her here the same night Shoshanna introduced me to her boyfriend. There was a party going on sponsored by the manufacturers of wood-heated hot tubs the owners of Forest used to sell.

Shoshanna may be at peace now, but this creature has already done her irreversible damage, as has the gray-bearded dick lurking at the gate. I'm abruptly aware of my heightened resentment toward these people, with whom an unknowing Shoshanna had been trustfully living and sleeping. I've been well acquainted with degenerates like these since my preteen years, having over-shared the stories of my run-ins with them till they've become about as true as urban legends. I used to think my tragic history was a potent pheromone, giving my gloomy disposition legs, rationalizing my offensive outbursts as uncontrollable manic episodes while I bragged about being bipolar, supposedly based on faulty genes and a troubled upbringing. I've often leveraged them to manipulate lovers into believing their lifelong vocation was to save me and only me till death do us part, instilling in them a fear of responsibility for my suicide should they ever make the wise, brave choice to escape the prison of our relationship. They're all gone now.

With her back to a line of sad mourners waiting for a refill, Amanda's "sneaking" a bump, the vial of cocaine poorly hidden in a crumpled tissue she's holding to her pointy nose. No one notices or cares. For the most part, Shoshanna's relatives are up-state country folk and former hippies, either clueless to the signs of drug use or still on them.

"Are you ready to go soon?" I ask Pedro, wondering if we'll run into the boyfriend on the street: he seems to have disappeared, or I just can't see him in the night.

"In a little bit. I want to spend more time with her family."

Drunken guests' voices rise in volume as darkness falls from the sky. Red Chinese lanterns hanging from the sheds turn on automatically. Nico's phone rings loudly, the disrupting light and sound adding to a transition in mood from a sad, quiet memorial service to a Sunday evening garden party.

"It's the ice delivery. They're already there," she says with a hint of urgency. She acts almost as if she were Pedro's manager, ensuring he's on time to events, keeping his commitments to deadlines. His excessive late-night partying and early-morning art-making often conflict with his work schedule. Dealing with logistical details seems to comfort her in her grief. A stereotypical Brit, she's not used to displaying emotions at all, let alone publicly. I can tell today is especially hard on her because she's acting all business.

"Relax. The gallerist will sign for it," he replies, slightly irritated. He wants to be generous with his time for Shoshanna, seem selfless—I know him all too well by now. But then he's rushing to say goodbye and we're heading for the exit. I don't say a word to anyone. At the gate, I see the boyfriend is definitely gone and am oddly disappointed.

ANOTHER MONOTONOUS MONDAY at White Advertising in Lower Manhattan, reading a company-wide email from the CEO, welcoming back from the weekend the one-thousand-plus employees who worked there, recapping the agency's many successes at Cannes, announcing a new business win—the music-streaming service Zeus—and the hiring of a new chief creative officer for North America. Deleting the message, I'd returned to my Facebook News Feed, saw a post from *Dazed* that linked to an interview of my best friend Pedro. He had an upcoming solo exhibition at Participant on the Lower East Side that would feature his paintings of "crying cocks" on used prescription bottles of Amoxicillin, documenting his brief breakup with Nico during which he'd engaged in countless unsafe sex acts and contracted chlamydia.

It was a big week for me: I was prepping to fire someone for the very first time. This wasn't something that brought me pleasure, despite the forthcoming termination of the slacking, ill-fitting individual being well deserved. The imminent confrontation would only add to the general anxiety disorder that's plagued me since childhood.

Following the same daily routine to this day, the predominantly male creatives at White maintain ballooned egos, but they lack the true artistic talent to warrant them—save for manipulating people into buying shit they don't need—as they do at most ad agencies. The majority sustain homoerotic bromances and synchronize their shit time. I'm talking actual shit, dozens upon dozens of meaty logs feeding the porcelain mouths in the restrooms on all fifteen floors of offices. The hipster buds, most with beards to substitute for a lack of personality, devour their lunches between 12:30 and 2PM every day, the movement of their bowels kicking in in tandem shortly thereafter, as evidenced by the lack of just one available stall in the whole building around that time.

After the CCO's promotion, he often joked about redesigning the executive conference room with wood paneling, a long marble table and toilets for seats—with fuzzy covers for comfort. He said he'd come up with every one of his award-winning campaign ideas on the toilet in his cabin upstate, so what better way to inspire the creatives! On the wall, behind the head of the table and his gold-plated toilet seat, he would hang a fine print of his own shit floating in the famed bowl. While it was said in jest, I wouldn't have been surprised if he'd gone through with it, considering his extreme arrogance and the sick sensibility of the ad industry.

To some, separating myself from the creatives' behavior might have seemed a bit contradictory, but they'd be wrong in their evaluation. I lived a double-life: Pedro allowed me access to the New York underground scene of artists and misfits who lived guiltless and carefree. It was my freedom. I convinced myself I was only working in the corporate world ironically. Used my pay to socialize with the "real" New York on weekends—parties, dinners, shows, et cetera—with another dimension of the city that refused to submit to the gentrification that was killing originality, diminishing the sense of danger and excitement that once characterized New York. Seeing the *Dazed* article made me proud of my friend, as if I were part of something special.

Pedro had dabbled in the corporate world as a designer for a Hasidic-owned company that mass-manufactured baby clothes. The monotony of a nine-to-five, wasting his talent on someone else's business, rotting in a cubicle when he could've been experiencing the world, having to tolerate the extremely conservative values of his employers and their censure, especially in the summer when he came to work underdressed, exposing his countless tattoos or having girls swing by for lunch in revealing outfits and with dogs in tow.

The last straw was when they fired his friend Jason, a fellow designer at the company who secretly revealed to Pedro he was transitioning to female. As her body slowly changed over the course of a year—breasts, longer hair, less weight, more feminine and tighter attire—the bosses grew suspicious until there was nothing Jason—now Jessica—could do other than admit the truth. And when she did, they threw up their hands in disgust and physically ejected her from the office.

Pedro's letter of resignation was sent after the office had cleared out for the night: giant posters of stills taken from a documentary showing gender reassignment surgery in graphic detail were super-glued to the walls of the bosses' offices. The police questioned Jessica about the vandalism, but she had an alibi. Pedro was my anti-hero. Made me invincible to the drudgeries of working in advertising and the ever-present Void of living in general.

PEDRO LOOKS THE same. His tan, naturally glowing skin, small frame and boyish smile lie about his age. With tiny teeth, albeit pot-stained, he gives the impression of never having graduated from the deciduous stage of dental development. Defying thirty-five years of age, he pretends to be fifteen years younger with lovers-slash-fans, not one of them questioning it. His South American genes and the youthful life he leads fool them all: moderately notorious, he gets by on somewhat frequent art sales, endless partying and casual fucking made doable by the most open relationship I've ever witnessed.

We were once inseparable, but we rarely see each other now. Tonight is the exception after six months because of Shoshanna's death and his show in a tiny pop-up gallery in Fort Greene a few blocks from my studio apartment—I've allowed him to use it as his dressing room. Inspired by seals coming ashore in record droves and sexually assaulting penguins, he's fastened makeshift tusks to his face using two skinny white dildos and a stretch of brown duct tape wrapped around his shaved, pea-shaped head— I've already told him that walruses grow tusks, not seals, but he insists his audience won't know the difference. Two clusters of broom straw jutting from the tape under his nostrils give him whiskers. His feet are booted in worn black combat boots, and he's naked under an army jacket with a bone-white shearling collar that Nico designed for Chris Krueger's gender-neutral autumn-slash-winter collection.

Crystal Castles soundtracks the pre-party at my apartment. Assorted tools of intoxication fuel the conversation, alleviating the awkwardness we all seem to be feeling. Overshadowed by the day's events and unexplained months Pedro's put between us, this reunion is not real: our hysterical laughter permeating the walls could be conjured by any drunks congregating.

Nico is thumbing through Tinder. Her bloodshot eyes are set in bleached-blond lashes that match her buzzed, zebra-streaked hair and pale, anorexic body dressed in black—that evergreen wardrobe choice we have in common. I used to love our street walks, both of us skinny and Goth, my virtually eternal state of depression meshing well with her British sensibility: an ability to display no emotion and a sense of humor drier than bone.

One on one with Pedro was always a much livelier affair. Not to say it was better, just different and more intimate. As an uncomfortable moment of silence intrudes on our little get-together, I sit here pot-dazed, gazing at a cloud of smoke hovering over the kitchen table and peering through it as Alice does her Looking Glass. What I see: meeting Pedro on the set of a MakeHer shoot for which he was commissioned to paint a mural entirely with MakeHer makeup on a glass wall we had constructed at the Williamsburg Waterfront. Thin late-teen actresses with collagen lips—one a transsexual—were styled as Brooklyn hipsters and meant to dance around it as if at a day rave. Rather than acquiescing to the brand's request that Pedro keep the artwork PG-13, he illustrated women hacking cocks off men and sewing them to each other's lips. I'd read about his work before we booked him for such a mass-market TV spot, warning the creatives it was a bad idea. They ignored me, feeling pressured to attract millennials to the aging makeup line. He was fired the second day and replaced by an imitation Keith Haring who charged an exorbitant fee. I found Pedro's bravado fascinating. We exchanged numbers and he quickly became my favorite person. And whereas he was my best friend for the next four years, I knew I wasn't his.

Marching across Willoughby to the gallery, Pedro, Nico and I turn the heads of a young Hasidic family, their identical twin babies in matching strollers shrieking at the sight of Pedro in his animal getup. Nico and I are trailing behind with black stockings pulled over our faces, which he insisted we wear to the show despite the stifling humidity. While the less open-minded have avoided him because of his blatant attention ploys, I've always found them rather stimulating. The more onlookers react—a group of boisterous brats from Pratt Institute screaming laughter, an Asian couple carrying groceries in reusable bags looking up from their Kindles in shock—the higher I get, proud to be a member of Pedro's crew, which I liken to a modern-day Warhol gang. I realize today is my final day in it—intuit this strongly—but ignore the sad fact for now, deciding to live in the moment, which has always been his prerogative.

WE'RE IN THE bleached hole, a tiny pop-up gallery on Myrtle—Nico and I drenched in sweat—a sliver of space between a juice shop and Chipotle, the walls painted white. Installed on them at eye-level are flat-screen TVs playing video art on a loop: blocks of sea ice breaking apart, the water on which it floats changing to molten lava. Screams of beasts in agony blare from a surplus of speakers stationed throughout the gallery.

A variety of outrageously dressed club kids decorate the room—I spot one in a Lydia-Deetz-style veil, neon blue piping spiraling around a nude body painted gold, an off-white faux shearling rug from Ikea repurposed as a kilt—as do the usual underground artists-slash-heavy-networkers, including Hugo, infamously risqué Slovakian photographer with whom I used to have late-night hookups. That is until the night he emerged from the bathroom in pink panties insisting it wasn't gay to go through his girlfriend's undies drawer while she was on holiday. Role-play has never been my thing. I've never been able to lose myself in the moment, pretend I'm someone else. My self-awareness is too formidable—I *did* allow him to photograph me nude a few times, but I refused to see the results; they'll likely be in his next monograph where I still won't look. Rushing by him when his back is turned, I pray he doesn't recognize my face underneath the pantyhose—he'll have other ideas for how to wear it.

This mix of nightlife personas and art freaks stems from Pedro having his hands in equal parts party promoting, painting and performance art. The events he puts together are works of art in themselves. He called the last one Fuck Your Mother. It featured a makeshift sex room in the basement of the Pyramid Club hung with plastic tarps and filled with cardboard boxes collected from abandoned homeless nests along Avenue A. The aroma of filthy vagrants and spontaneous sex was as overpowering as the ammonia in cat piss. The deep house music and Pedro's *a capella* solo about visualizing his estranged father when ejaculating on coke was great, though. I didn't end up getting fucked by anyone myself, but I would've without reserve had I found someone I fancied.

Other than occasionally whispering catty comments to Nico, I remain speechless in a corner about ten feet from the "stage," a five-by-six slab of ice six inches thick. Everyone's assuming we're part of the installation anyway, so they're not talking to us. A white screen hangs just behind the stage. I can see Pedro on the other side of it painting naked, emaciated men and women black and white.

"When's he going on?"

"Soon. He was waiting for the rest of the performers to get here."

"Then maybe we should get closer."

Nico chuckles. "Um, no. I was going to suggest moving back."

"Why?" I ask, to no response.

Pedro and his costumed friends rush the stage, the misfit crowd cheering in unison. His painted troupe of performers croaks, arms close to either side of their bodies, slapping their thighs with pitch-black-painted hands. He lets out a great roar, which prompts the others to slap more violently.

The growling and smacking sounds reverberate through The Bleached Hole and out onto the half-gentrified streets: looking past the indoor audience, I see a group of tall giggling black and Latino teens dressed for the basketball court have collected at the entrance to the gallery, along with an overweight elderly white man wobbling on his cane and a lesbian couple holding hands.

Pedro grabs one of his nearly anorexic helpers by the back of the neck and forces her onto the ice belly down. He gets on his knees and throws the Krueger coat off his shoulders, revealing a stiff cock—quite thick and long for such a small body. Without lubrication, he violently shoves inside his pretend victim's asshole. While the others onstage croak in disagreement, the actress he's fucking screams in what sounds like genuine pain. With a Chewbacca groan Pedro pulls out and shoots into the audience, some of it getting on the cheek of an unsuspecting Hugo standing too close to the stage. Nico nudges me, saying through a chuckle, "That's why." Hugo, who vehemently maintains a masculine public image, shrieks effeminately, and the crowd, who was silent during the attack, erupts into laughter.

Pedro takes a bow as the rest of the cast assists the "assaulted" one behind the screen, leaving on the melting ice little drops of blood. The crowd goes berserk as if at a sporting event. Feeling detached and on drugs and having long ago been desensitized to Pedro's art, I drift my focus to the other side of the screen. With Wet Ones his helpers are wiping body paint off their limbs, obscenely satisfied smiles spreading across their faces, including Pedro's costar.

FOUR YEARS: THE countless moments all a blur, a dizzying blend of paint, performances, psychedelic drugs, outrageous people and loud music. My memory has consolidated our great friendship into one big night out. I can empathize with seniors who have trouble seeing the date and timestamp on past experiences, people they've known who've long ago passed, loves and friendships lost yesterday or decades ago. But if I could just stick my hand in my swirling brain, pull out one or two memories like slippery goldfish from a bowl... there we go:

Had eaten shrooms at Forest with Pedro but they didn't seem to be working, so I headed home to sleep, had an early morning meeting anyway. Walked into my apartment, saw my Shiba Inu Max surrounded by light, felt such appreciation for this sentient being that suddenly represented pure life. As I lay in bed holding him, staring into his heavenly, wise black eyes, a translucent cartoon of Hell played in front of mine: a red, fiery world complete with goofy goblins and a bulging-eyed Satan with curled horns and a veneered smile. My funny Paradise Lost hallucination came to a screeching halt—a needle scratching a record—when Pedro rang.

"Hello?"

Dead silence.

"Pedro, are you there?"

More silence.

"Okay, maybe you butt-dialed me."

"Am I bad a person?" he whispered.

"What?"

"What if it's all wrong?" he sobbed. "Maybe I shouldn't be living like this."

"No, what do you mean?" I forced myself into sobriety so I could be there for him. "You're everything, you're... people love you. What you do is brave. Your art... I wish I had half the courage you do..."

"Okay," he sniveled.

"Where are you?"

"... In the hallway of my building, I think... didn't want to wake Nico."

"Well, go in and try to sleep."

"I pissed myself."

"What!" I chuckled. "Do you want me to come there?"

"No... no. You're right, I'm gonna go."

Dropped the phone on the bed, turned to my doggy. I'd never witnessed Pedro in such a self-pitying state. He was the King of Shamelessness, the Sultan of Sin and proud of it. It didn't turn me off per se, just confused me, turned the tables: with temporarily deranged senses I was in tune with myself, with life, and appreciated who I was and what I had, while he had turned into the sober version of me: uncertain, insecure and a little psychotic. Still, I'd been the one in whom he'd chosen to confide his fears, expose his vulnerability.

BY MIDNIGHT NICO has departed—she never breaks work-night curfew—leaving Pedro to me with my age-old promise of taking over as chaperone, helping to break down the show, ensuring he's in a cab before daybreak. He's nearly cross-eyed, rubbing one of the white dildos that had been taped to his face against the ass of a naked cast member, a girl known as Dumpster Diva, who has attached the other dildo to a leather strap-on and is flopping it around as she backs into him. Dumpster Diva has a strong overbite and a large Instagram following, executing regular scavenger hunts for discarded, expired food outside Whole Foods and Trader Joe's, snapping pics of her half-spoiled findings and pushing them to her feed. Later, she makes "gourmet" meals and shares photos of them, too.

I used to bring lovers around to meet Pedro while he was intoxicated like this, with comparable crowds of extreme misfits. After all, he is—or was—my best friend. In my opinion, introducing them to Pedro was a test to see if the relationships could turn into something serious. Without fail they either left immediately in disgust or never considered me more than a party buddy from then on. "We don't have the same values," one of them breakup-texted. I took it as a compliment, relished the rejection.

In truth, at the time I only wanted to be with Pedro anyway, despite the nonsexual nature of our relationship.

We'd had a romp on an MDMA holiday in Berlin, confusing platonic love for romance, but it didn't go anywhere. Getting to bed in his friend's flat at noon after a two-day binge at Berghain, we made out, cuddled, felt each other up and down. Sadly, our bodies didn't match: he's small-framed and soft-skinned, a physicality that doesn't sync with my unhealthy, unrealistic sexual needs. His ego was bruised till we fell unconscious. The next day we were back to normal but with an unspoken acknowledgement of the limits to our love. And I did love him, greatly, just as I have every one of my lost lovers. I still do, regardless of the extent to which he's pulled out of Us these last several months for reasons never explained.

Perhaps the end began at the start of our last holiday alone together: a jaunt in Amsterdam over Memorial Day weekend, my plans for a coupled visit to the Van Gogh, a paired cycle tour on clunky rented bikes, a boat cruise for two on the city's dark, narrow canals. "Tourism is for sheep," he had argued, which I happen to agree with, but it could've been funny to experience it ironically with him. I already knew he didn't like museums. He says they cloud his creativity, but his rejection of that kind of activity is really a symptom of his inferiority complex: his works have yet to graduate from the New York underground art scene to more mainstream heights—if they ever will. He was only in Amsterdam for the nightlife, networking and fucking. Left me at a club to join a college-age five-some in a youth hostel, gave me an Irish goodbye. I suppose I was expecting him to take some responsibility for my devotion, of which only a lover is capable, and even with them it's asking too much: my insatiable desperation for someone, something, *anything* to fill the nauseating Void. Sheep life doesn't seem so bad compared to living painfully self-aware.

Or our friendship might have soured like a Dumpster Diva feast the time when I produced one of his music videos. I'd been overwhelmed with the new MakeHer account, which unsurprisingly had one hell of a demanding client: beauty advertising commands flawlessness. I'd been spending the majority of my real-job days producing three TV commercials simultaneously, scouring New York and Los Angeles for immaculate models who could act, celebrity hairstylists and makeup artists, acclaimed directors of photography who could light skin pristinely and directors on whom both the client and creatives could passionately agree, praying they were available for virtually next-day shoots, obliging purse-pinched budgets and unreasonable post-production deadlines. But when Pedro asked me to partner with him on a project, I eagerly accepted. I had never allowed myself to be an artist but was hell-bent on transcending the station I'd been born into—which is why it's difficult fathoming why my older brother and his new family are happily settled in the lower-middle-class world. Associating myself with free people—painters, performers, writers, and the like—who choose to live on the fringes of society and suffer economically for their art has satiated my creative urges, however vicariously.

Music video for "Donkey Punchin' Nun" from Pedro's then-forthcoming album *The Holy Rape Tape*:

Talent: Fans 1-3 Pedro was fucking
Director of Photography/Camera Operator: Hugo
Key Grip: Fan 4 Pedro was fucking
Gaffer: Fan 5 Pedro was fucking
Best Boy: Fan 6 Pedro was fucking
Hair & Makeup: Ms. STD Scripts (club-kid superstar who also cuts hair at Patricia Field's)
Wardrobe: Nico
Set Design: Pedro
Original Music: Pedro
Location: Pedro and Nico's flat
Producer: Me
Writer: Pedro
Director: Pedro

Synopsis: The scene opens on a close-up of Pedro singing, slowly pulling out to reveal him shirtless, torso painted white, heavy black makeup under his eyes to effect a dead look, the lyrics clarifying that he's the "Holy Ghost of Assholes." As the song progresses, the camera zooms out farther to reveal him naked, fucking one of three "nuns" bent over before him in the ass. Each is on hands and knees waiting for a turn with Pedro's cock, naked save for the habits on their heads that Nico has designed—she'd tricked the seamstresses at Chris Krueger to make them as part of the label's forthcoming collection.

Adding to the chaos of a tiny one-bedroom packed with camera equipment and a fire-violation number of people, Pedro allowed another film crew to capture behind-the-scenes footage for a Dutch reality show about the wild lives of up-and-coming artists from around the globe. At some point during the shoot he'd grown tired of my keeping everyone on script and following the shot list so we could finish on schedule—basically my job on set as the producer—and into my beer he dropped a few crystals of pure MDMA concocted by a chemistry major in a lab at MIT. Blacked out. Couldn't remember what had happened until I found the reality show episode online a month later: a sweat-sopped, eye-popping me crawling through a forest of legs, eventually finding a home at the feet of Dee Dee Heinz, the man behind the hipster-popular R&B electronica band Plasma Peach, who let me station beneath him curled up like a cat, likely less out of kindness than to project an air of being too cool to acknowledge such a mess.

"We don't work well together," was Pedro's excuse for drugging me when I finally confronted him.

"I was doing what you asked me to do: *produce*," I argued. "The whole thing was chaos. If you wanted to play dictator instead of director you shouldn't have brought me on. Two of those fans you cast as nuns didn't even know fucking was part of the deal and only agreed to it after you got them high."

"Look, I'm not going to sit here and explain my creative process to someone like you. You wouldn't understand 'cause you live life under the corporate sun. You're *not* an artist! Part of the piece was making them my creation. Didn't you read my *Interview* interview?!" Two stripes of tears paralleled down my face. He gave me a look of disgust in response. "I'm starting to think I made a mistake by bringing you into my life. I'm saying goodbye to this discussion forever," he announced and ended the call.

Forcibly collecting my hurt, I texted, *I'll see you at the show tonight, okay? / This can't come between us / You're my favorite person, the only person in my life…* utterly terrified as I was that he'd left me for good. At the show—a sobering opening night for a collection of paintings he'd been trying to market mainstream that ended up with the worst reviews of his career—kissed my cheek sloppily, praised me for coming and said he missed me, as if nothing had happened. I pretended the same, grateful and excited about his forgiveness.

Eliminating the memory of the music video shoot from my mind, I turn my focus to The Bleached Hole, dismantling televisions from its walls while Pedro fucks Dumpster Diva behind the white screen. The crowd has dispersed, is heading home for a few hours of sleep before work tomorrow or the basement of the Dream Hotel in Manhattan for an after-hours, which I doubt either Pedro or I will make because the drugs are back at my flat. I have a 9AM meeting coming up, but just a couple more hours, I vow to myself, promising to cut off our one-night holiday at 2AM.

Flat for *apartment* or *holiday* for *vacation* or *cycle* for *bike* are among other choice nuances of the British vernacular that I've borrowed from Nico. Not to mention my assumption of Pedro's character, every trick and trade he's purposed to rattlesnake-charm me and own the attention of anyone in his radius no matter the social situation. Making lovers a part of me when I lose them is my way of healing—things like wearing their signature scent, mimicking their clothing style or adopting an infectious laugh and disarming smile—settling for the dregs of missed-out futures with ex-Us's.

MY THIRTY-EIGHT-YEAR-OLD OLDER brother Mickey had materialized from an Uber with a freshly shaved head and perfectly ironed Oxford shirt, no doubt courtesy of his pregnant wife Tara. She'd allowed him a night out in the city—*he deserves a little break,* she'd texted me earlier in the night, *for putting up with my hormonal mood swings eek!*—with the promise he'd return Sunday afternoon for their next Lamaze class. Over six feet tall, he looked down at me with brown oval eyes, a handsome smile and shiny forehead. To me he was just average in the looks department, but in urban Connecticut he'd always snagged the prettiest girls in high school. His warm personality and levelheaded demeanor might've had something to do with it too. The regular-fit jeans he was wearing looked as if they hadn't been washed in a few days and were slightly frayed at the bottom. On his feet were cheap boat shoes likely from Payless or somewhere comparable.

"You look great!" I told him sincerely. Toiling away seven days a week to save for the baby, he was usually in dirty construction gear: faded work pants and old sweatshirts stained with paint and covered in sawdust.

"Thanks," he smiled, bear-hugging me. "Tara said I clean up nicely, too... so what's the plan tonight?"

"We're going to Pedro's party, remember? Excited for you to meet him." I had a huge smile on my face with wide-open eyes, as if they'd pop out of their sockets at any moment.

"You sure started the party early," he said, sounding concerned and slightly annoyed.

"What do you mean?"

"Um… your jaw won't stop clenching and your hands are shaking… hope you're not like this all the time."

"Aw, come on! We're celebrating! … I stopped at the venue to help Pedro set up and did a little pre-gaming. Anyway, you said you wanted to rage tonight."

"Yeah… maybe a little later. It's only seven… thought we'd grab dinner first."

"I'll get dinner, we can get dinner, yeah, let's go, I know a place." My legs were stiff as we walked down Bedford Avenue, knees practically unbending. I couldn't tell if it was from the gym earlier in the day or because I was high on coke. Either way, I hoped he didn't notice. When I turned back to him, he was several feet behind—not used to walking like a New Yorker—and he seemed to be staring at me in a funny way, but it could've been my paranoia. We settled on a Thai restaurant. Despite my extreme lack of appetite, I was determined to eat with my brother.

When Mickey and I finally reached the club, Pedro was hanging off Nico, who was working as the door girl. Mickey was a little buzzed from a few pints of IPA at the restaurant, so he was more open to having a little fun—we'd also had a few bumps in the cab ride from Brooklyn.

"Pedro, meet my brother Mickey."

"Ah, the famous Mickey. I've heard so little about you," he joked. Went to shake Mickey's hand, but the extension of his arm made him lose his balance and tip over, forcing both of them to the ground. On top of Mickey, Pedro was laughing hysterically.

"Get up, get off me, dude!"

"Pedro!" Nico scolded like a mother, pulling him to his feet. "I'm so sorry about this."

"Sorry," I mouthed to Mickey, shrugging.

"Come inside," Pedro moaned. "I'll get you guys some party favors." It was his way of apologizing. Maintaining a wobbly stance, he led us through a plastic tarp hanging over the doorway so no one could see the sin inside.

Debauchery: by ten a couple was already fucking in the corner; all I could make out in the dark was a bare ass clenching and unclenching as it pumped into someone and two long legs with high-heeled feet wrapped around it. Open-mouthed in a frozen stance, Mickey stared with unblinking eyes.

"What is this place?" he asked.

"It's Fuck My Mother, one of Pedro's theme parties.

"Ah."

The bartender was thin and topless, with saggy tits. Pedro ordered a couple beers for us and then whispered into the bartender's ear. After he gave her one of his irresistible winks and a kiss on the cheek, she topped off the beers with what I assumed was MDMA, shaking granules into the bottles from a tiny salt-shaker.

"Here you go, fam!" Pedro said, handing us the beers, spilling some. "I'll be black, you stay white here."

"What the hell was that?" Mickey asked. He leaned against the bar and straightened; then leant back again: the coke was speedy.

"Pretty sure it's MDMA. That's what it usually is... just drink it."

Separated from the crowd in a dark corner, I witnessed the rest through close-knit mesh: fragmented images of dancing bodies, laughing faces; Pedro swinging his dick around to equal measures of cheers and jeers; Nico standing idly by with arms crossed, her platinum hair pristinely coiffed despite the cloud of perspiration hanging over the club; the stench of cock, pussy, piss and other body odors intensified by the drugs; my brother in the corner getting blown by a girl who may have not been one at birth—but he couldn't tell the difference, because he was much higher than I was. I couldn't remember the last time he'd done drugs, if ever.

We awoke fully clothed late the next afternoon. Max had taken a shit in the apartment because by then I hadn't let him out for thirty-six hours, and Mickey had vomited on himself during the night. There were ten missed calls from his wife. He'd slept through Lamaze.

"What happened last night? I feel like I'm dying."

"Yeah, me too. I don't even remember how we got home, do you?"

"Fuck, Tara is freaking out. Can you order me a cab? Gotta get on the train now." He grabbed his wallet and keys and was calling her back on his way out.

"It was nice to see you," I said, feeling guilty for dragging him down the rabbit hole, for taking advantage of his need to relieve the stress of a baby on the way with our family blood coursing through it.

"Yeah. Talk soon, love—hey, baby?" The door shut, and his voice was muffled until it faded away as he jetted down the hall to the elevators.

The next day he sent me a text saying he was really worried about me. He felt sick about what we'd done. I shouldn't be hanging around a guy like Pedro. He could see how obsessed I was with our friendship and combined with drugs it could only end badly. He didn't want to see me hurt myself again. I loved him for caring, but I brushed off the concern, told him everything was and would be fine, that Pedro was bringing me out of my shell. Mickey was well aware of how alone I'd been, the depression I'd battled for years, so he didn't contest any further, knew it wouldn't have done any good and was likely just preparing himself to be there when I fell again.

A MILD WEEKNIGHT rager is the best—maybe the only—way to end Pedro's and my friendship. At my side he drags his petite body across Myrtle, a drunk zombie, no Krueger jacket. He's forgotten it back at the gallery, and Nico will be furious tomorrow, but when is she not? And she won't say anything, no, she'll keep it all inside with the rest of her mixed feelings until she implodes or explodes, likely the former.

Dumpster Diva has petered out a few blocks back. She found her place on the corner of Clinton and Myrtle and jiggled her stuff like a West Side Highway hooker from the '90s, slapping her pale thighs with the floppy, bone-white dildo strapped to her waist. A police car speeds past us with sirens and lights on. I'm thinking someone may have called the cops on her. She's certainly a sight tonight: intoxicated and dressed in a thin, hot-pink bikini bottom with the strap-on over it, her flat adolescent-boy chest unapologetically topless, although it *is* legal in this city for a woman to expose her breasts in public. Responding to a slight feeling of responsibility for her, I rush a discreet key bump between passing pedestrians and cars to escape the guilt of leaving her behind.

"Gimme one," Pedro drawls, tapping the tip of my nose with a limp hand.

"We're almost there," I deny consolingly, the streets having suddenly busied themselves with a line of suspicious cars crawling in the opposite direction. A black runway-style couple crosses our path with side-wise glances, sharing the burden of a massive blue Ikea bag overstuffed with clean, perfectly folded laundry—I didn't know the Laundromat over there was open twenty-four hours because there are machines in my building. A midnight jogger gives Pedro the stink eye, and a pizza delivery man of ambiguous ethnicity is locking up one of those obnoxious electric bikes with an old rusty chain, which my paranoid brain is likening to a serial killer's favorite restraint. Pedro trips on a deformed square of sidewalk, dropping his iPhone with the Tinder app brightening its screen.

"You cracked it bad," I say, picking it up and handing it over. "Didn't Nico just replace this?"

"It's all good," he says nonchalantly. "It's just the future fighting back."

"Yeah," I agree, chuckling mildly—though his argument isn't clear to me—knowing tomorrow's sober version of him will add this to the list of why our friendship is damaging.

Hung over last summer on a sweltering Sunday night after a two-day binge, Pedro and I had been on top of his and Nico's building, sticky tar gluing our bare torsos to the roof's surface as we lay on our bellies, heads bent over the edge, gazing glassy-eyed at the street life below. "I'm gonna take a break now, like a long one, at least a month," he said, "focus on my art," as if I were the one influencing him to throw his infamously debauched soirees keeping us up forty-eight-plus hours almost every weekend. "Don't be a little bitch," he'd jibe whenever I'd try to exit for sleep. Not that I'm blaming him for anything. The decision to indulge in our arguably self-destructive behavior has always been mine: I've never felt more alive than when we were together, in any situation or state of mind. "We've been dancing too close to the Edge of Darkness," he said that night, "and if we don't take a step back we'll destroy ourselves… everything we've worked for and love."

Maybe he was right, but I loved no one but him. Our clear-headed time together consisted mainly of talks about recovering from the weekend and upcoming parties—it was Nico and I who found commonalities in the superficialities of "real life" because we both had "real jobs." But just because Pedro and I weren't sober when we were intimate doesn't mean our love wasn't real. As with Shoshanna, when Pedro's and my senses were deranged temporarily it freed us from our virtually countless demons: ugly, monstrous creatures living lonely in our ears, influencing us to torture our bodies and hurt others—and me to choose physically and mentally violent lovers—to fuck the pain away; demons from whom we knew we'd never be separated.

WHEN PEDRO WAS seven, his mother moved illegally with him to the U.S., leaving his father to rot in an Ecuadoran prison. The father had drunkenly beaten a man to death with a crowbar for mouthing off when he bumped into him on the street— "*Puto!*" Settling them down in Queens, his mother sold herself for cash and crack after realizing America didn't come with the dream as advertised.

In Pedro's teen years he immersed himself in the skateboarding scene, forming tight bonds with street hustlers, competing at illegal rinks throughout the five boroughs, guzzling cheap booze every night and selling weed to Manhattanites. His most frequent customer was Ron Sax, one of the elite American contemporary artists who'd had his creative hands in several art forms: sculpture, painting, music and performance. He and Pedro became fast friends in a pseudo father-slash-son relationship, and in less than a year Pedro abandoned his mother and the crack den in which he'd been raised for Ron's East Village floor-through co-op apartment on Avenue A.

I had only met Ron once, during the first month of my friendship with Pedro—the beginning of our four-year intimacy incomparable to his relationship with anyone else, including Nico and Ron. By then Ron was already in his infamous wheelchair, the inanimate object acting almost as a muse, half his face drooping a centimeter or two more than the other. At least two or three times a month that led up to his suicide, *Page Six* published a photo of him and a newly designed chair. His first piece, *Just Stroked*, consisted of soup cans painted black, tied with catgut to the frame of the backrest, dragging along the ground noisily as he rolled through Tompkins Square Park, a cow heart sliced into pieces sitting on his permanently numb thighs. Pedro introduced us, and Ron just nodded, treating me as if I were one of Pedro's fans and this was a temporary fling—probably because he was jealous.

When Pedro had first moved in with him, there'd been a lot of parties for Pedro and friends, drugs brought out on silver trays. Several late mornings, Ron had tried blowing an incoherent Pedro, once or twice succeeding. But Pedro never confronted Ron about it, rationalizing that it was a small price to pay for living in a real home.

Ron left his apartment to his sister and around fifty grand to Pedro, which he blew through in less than a year on extravagant warehouse parties in secret locations throughout Brooklyn, often attended by celebrities and artists he'd met through Ron—subsequently making a name for himself in the New York underground, with exposés about him in *Interview*, *Dazed*, *Paper*, *Time Out* and *Vogue*, to name a few.

Our family histories—not to mention our natural propensity for hustling—had clear parallels: our fathers had committed murder, albeit for different reasons; both of our parents had been or

still were addicts of various substances. And when we were together, our comparably awful pasts canceled out, two negatives
equaling a positive, if only temporarily.

I WISH PEDRO would lift the drooping lids over his deep-seeing eyes, realize how reductively he evaluates Us, appreciate what we've built and what he's relinquishing permanently. Instead, the junk mail I pulled from the box on our way inside my building is his focus: a Geico promotional letter offering 15%-or-more savings on car insurance. I haven't owned a car in eleven years. With a dying black Sharpie he's scribbling a portrait of my likeness on the envelope, then rubbing in a mixture of cigarette ash and cocaine—how dare he waste it!—a warlock's brew of the End of Us. The clock reads three, but it's really four because I haven't gotten around to shifting the hour hand for daylight savings time.

Having excused myself to the bathroom without his acknowledging it, I run the faucet on high to silence my ensuing defecation, as if the telltale smell won't rat me out anyway.

Back at the table he's sucked into the screen on my white MacBook, somehow able to operate the machine like a pro despite his otherwise unplugged state.

"Sold!"

"What?"

"Do you have Saran Wrap or a plastic bag or something?"

Over his shoulder I see he's posted a pic of the drawing he made less than five minutes ago to Facebook: *The Black Hole. Black marker with cigarette ash and cocaine on a business-size envelope. Contact privately for sales.* In a message overlay he's sharing his PayPal information with a goober in Belgium who's promptly purchased the piece for two thousand euros.

"Good for you."

"It's whatever."

The deal settled, he consciously joins me in the room for the first time, but it's too late: white lines of coke have been deleted, last drops of beer trickled down throats. The familiar threat of daybreak is pushing through the blinds, and I have work in a few hours.

"I can't believe I've been sitting here this long," he says.

"What do you mean? We've been catching up."

"What time is it? Shit, Nico went home alone…"

"When has she ever been pissed you're with me?"

He's rummaging through the kitchen like a raccoon, searching in vain for plastic wrap or a bag to protect *The Black Hole*, his palpable regret and resentment toward me gaining strength with each sobering slam of a cabinet door.

"Wait, I have something." I grab a roll of Max's poop bags hidden under a pile of black laundry and toss it to him. Among the dirty clothes: a T-shirt stained with a random hookup's come and a couple socks stuck together with bloody snot from my being too hung over to leave bed to blow my coke-congested nose.

"Thanks," he says ungratefully, tearing off a shit bag and outfitting his art with it. "I'm gonna head." His announcement elevates my already trembling extremities to late-stage Parkinson's.

"Really? Couldn't you stay a little longer? As long as I get like three hours of sleep before work I'll be fine. I haven't seen you in forever. Or you can stay ov—"

"I have a big day of painting tomorrow," he says flatly. "Can you get me an Uber on your phone? I don't have the app."

"I need to ask you something." He sits back down, lays the wrapped art on the table and begins smoothing the wrinkled plastic.

"What's up, what is it."

"Well, it's just…" I hesitate and then spit it out like a nervous teen: "Nico sent me a Facebook invite to your birthday party, but you blocked me from it." He sighs heavily, looks up at me: a shaken tree with tears instead of fruit falling loose. "I know we've grown apart," I go on, "but both you and Nico have been my close friends for years. I certainly haven't been a *perfect* friend, but I don't get what I've done that was so terrible you want nothing to do with me now. And it's not about the party. I don't care about the party." He turns his ocular attention to Max, who's nudging his shins with a furry toy, but Pedro ignores him.

"Listen, I'm gonna be honest. Yes, I uninvited you to my birthday party, but it's not meant to hurt you. I just forgot to tell Nico when she started planning everything. You and I both know it would've been too weird having you there. I only brought you on tonight out of respect for Shoshanna and the connection we all had… once upon a time.

"As far as why I don't want to be friends anymore, that's harder to explain. The only way I can explain it is, I see a black hole. And black holes are destructive. I have my own self-destructive tendencies, so we're not a good match. Maybe some friendship could've been restored, but you nailed the last nail in the coffin by continuing a friendship with my girlfriend when I obviously needed space from you. That's just me being honest, since you asked. Can you call me a cab now?"

"For... the... record," I say, tapping on my phone for a car. "It wasn't a stra-strategic move to stay friends with her after we stopped talking, okay? I... I thought I was friends with both of you. Didn't know I wasn't allowed to see her... I know, I *know* what you mean by us feeding off of each other's bad habits, but come on, there's much more to our... friendship... than that." A bell-like sound tolls from my phone, the volume of which is on high. "The car is here," I mumble.

His lips are shaking mildly, but unlike me, he's keeping his high under control. Scooping up his screen-cracked phone and coke-encrusted keys, he gives me a goodbye-forever look, a sympathetic "Take care of yourself" for the sad shadow of a person before him, and heads for the door.

"Don't go, okay? I'm sorry... I can be a better friend! We don't need to do drugs anymore, just..."

But he's still walking toward the door as my brain scans my mind for something—anything—to keep him here. Suddenly he freezes mid-step and falls forward, his forehead slamming into the corner of the plastic kitchen table. He collapses to the floor, a tiny pool of blood forming under his head, every coked-up beat of my heart instantly interrogating me: *What did you do? Did you kill him! You fed him drugs and stressed him out with your insane desperation! If he overdosed it's on you!*

"I... I'm sorry. Just stay..." I can feel myself zoning out, the world around me steaming up like windows of a car hosting a hot fuck. I hear Max's muffled whimpering as I begin to go deaf from shock, see his blurry figure lapping up Pedro's blood.

The cabbie's calling my phone. Sending him to voicemail I thumb to the app, canceling the ride. I hardly hear his angry beeping outside and the car screeching away, as if I'm wearing earplugs. Shooing the dog, I lie beside my best friend rather than calling 911, can't let him go. Try to force my gaze through his lidded eyes, anxiety abating, coke high seeping from my bones. Drape a quivering arm across his body, remembering how many times this bitch of a drug blocked me from sleep and peace of mind, but never with him.

"There's nothing to be paranoid about. No one's coming, not when I'm here with you... just sleep," he'd say softly. I'd be eternally grateful for his presence, for keeping me safe from solitude and the Coke Boogeyman those late mornings.

"You're my best friend, okay?" I'd reply to his snoring. "I love you so much."

ME, IMMORTAL TEENAGER: always awkward and anxious, forever lonely, constantly desirous of Yes's from No's as if I were the deserving exception. Was somehow owed Yes because I came from No. Relentless tantrums when I didn't get my way. Threatening suicide in vain. Blaming murder on my parents' mortal sins since my eleventh birthday to my present thirties. Oh, the countless privileges my grief has afforded me!

I'm still grounded in the bedroom of my Goth teen years, kneeling before a makeshift altar, fervently whispering a Wiccan prayer, pointing at the night sky in the window with a silver-plate athame, its blade stained with blood from my inner arms: I'm casting a dark spell on Him, in whichever of the many forms He's assumed this time: quarterback of Fairfield Prep, skinhead with chipped front tooth, balding dermatologist, coked-up lawyer, older entrepreneurial married Mormon, hedge fund banker with anger management issues, drugged-out DJ-slash-bartender, Pedro the street artist. I light the Black Candle.

FROM THIS DENSELY fogged distance the gates to Forest materialize magically like the secret entrance to a biblical heaven in the clouds. A weeping willow living lonely just inside the lot makes for a pathetic guardian to Paradise, its limp branches sobbing over rusty bars. I'm walking north on Kent in my signature black. My black hooded windbreaker keeps a delicate but annoying rain from intolerant me. These puffy, darkly circled eyes are hiding behind mist-covered Warby Parker glasses and a couple layers of MakeHer concealer. Under black umbrellas, obedient nine-to-fivers with Monday-glum faces are hurrying in the opposite direction. I have a silly thought that they're leaving Shoshanna's service, but of course that was yesterday—I'm on one to two hours of sleep, so my brain is operating at fifty-five percent maximum.

Begrudgingly walk to where I began last night, to my bike at the nursery. Can't count how many times I've drunkenly abandoned it somewhere in Brooklyn or downtown Manhattan, often forgetting where I'd left it. At least this time I remember: it's locked to a stop sign near Forest. This is the end of my journey, the End of Us. I can see the matte black finish of my Trek glistening in the rain the closer I get. A lumpy black mass of what I assume is garbage lies beside it.

As old as I am, I'm surprised I still have it in me: the strength to rise from such a deadly indulgent evening to make a 9AM meeting. But I'm a professional. An ad person. My Poor Richard-ness is the only thing keeping me from suffocating myself to death with a plastic grocery bag from the un-gentrified C-Town around the corner; instead of using them to commit suicide, I use them as poop bags for Max, my sole contribution to recycling.

A section of my psyche imagines how different now would be with Shoshanna as a partner to my freshly committed crimes. I finger the curled card from her service in my front right pocket, which I'd used as a nose straw a few hours ago. The sight of her hauntingly cheerful face printed on it conjures a sunny day in con-tradiction to this gray, hung-over morning. In truth, she was never that happy. I recollect that magnetic smile as if she were spreading her lips in real time, but not as most would. Shoshanna was a Corazón on the rocks, no chaser, her happiness limited to the amount of its intake—I'm a whiskey lover myself; tequila draws out the anger in me so I rarely imbibe it. If she were alive and tagging along, the circumstances would be about the same, but her hysterical company, and our demons encircling us in a wild game of Duck, Duck, Goose, would make it seem a little better.

Better than now: as I near a man on the rained-on, pissed-on, spat-on sidewalk. He's asleep or dead before the gates to Forest, his back to me. Curb for pillow, my bike front tire as headboard. Metropolitan deathbed. Breathing or not, he's close to *some* end, surrounded by Monday morning, white worker bees nonchalantly passing by. The very audacity of his highly public indignity, conscious or not! Not needing civilized societal manners stops him from existing, save for acting as the disgusting warning sign he is. Parts of me are envious. He groans.

"Hey, you're on my bike."

Dead man's head turns: Shoshanna's boyfriend!

"I know you... Fuck me, what fucking time is it?"

"It's morning. You're on my bike."

Walking around to the front of him, I interrupt the brisk stride of a young professional, his long hair in a man bun.

"Watch it," says the man.

"Oh, fuck off," I say.

The guy keeps going, and the boyfriend is laughing into a coughing spasm. He's dressed in black: torn black T-shirt, wide-legged black jeans darker in the crotch—piss, likely. His classic Timberlands are scuffed, complementing the deep lines in his forehead, gray skin and hair. In the air the once-gentle patter of rain is coming into its own, the miniscule drops of water fattening up and falling heavier.

"Are you okay," I say with faked concern. Need to get on my bike: my common hangover cure, and precipitation bothers me less when I'm riding in it. The commute to the office will act as yet another baptism, washing away my latest sins against lovers and friends. Help me forget them all before I lose my mind again. As many times as I've made them and lost them and collected new Us's, and then killed them all over again, something tells me that Pedro was the grand finale. Realization sets in as the boyfriend gets on all fours, and then latches two fingers onto the slippery wet handlebars of the bike, trying to stand. Losing his grip, he falls back to the ground, landing on his stubbly chin.

"Motherfucker!" he yowls sobbingly. Blood runs from his face. "What did I do? Oh god, what did I do? Shoshanna. Shoshanna…"

This could be a drunken confession about taking her life or just guilt for enabling her alcoholism, beating the shit out of her countless times, having that crack whore Amanda—among many others, I'm sure—suck on his wrinkly old cock, which I saw on Shoshanna's iPhone during one of our demonic Show-and-Tell's in the shed inside Forest. I'm wondering if I should record his rambling and send it to the detective on her case, but he's being too vague. I doubt it'd hold up in court. Arresting him wouldn't do her rotting body any good, anyway.

"Come on," I say. "Just come on."

Kneeling, I yank his left arm over my shoulder and pull him to his feet, my strength surprising me considering how unrested I am. With the black T-shirt I'm wearing I wipe the tears, snot and blood from his face, making him wince. He pushes me away forcefully. My ill-fitting eyeglasses almost slip off my nose.

"Aw just leave me the fuck alone. You don't know me! You don't know what I've done!… They wouldn't let me see her! I just wanted to see my baby!"

"She wasn't there. It was a memorial service."

"Wha…?"

"They buried her upstate like two weeks ago."

He scoffs at his stupidity, a "why" look on his face, his eyes pleading with the wet sky.

Pulling the keyring for my bike lock from my pocket, I notice another key that opens the side door to Forest. The owners gave it to me yesterday to set up the memorial, install the collages with Pedro and Nico and stock the bar. A half-finished baggie of blow is floating gracefully to the ground—luckily there's no one on the street at the moment. I curse myself for not checking my jeans earlier. Pedro would've stayed with Us if I'd had more drugs, would've kept at bay the permanent loneliness a little longer. But through the fog I see the white of a police car driving toward us. The boyfriend and I must look insanely suspicious: coke on the ground, my hung-over pallor, the boyfriend dripping blood and cursing the air.

"We've gotta move!" Snatching the blow, I march toward Forest, taking hold of the boyfriend's upper arm on the way.

"Fuck are you doing!" he protests, struggling to break free.

"Cops are heading, and I'm not about to be arrested with you." His resistance instantly ceases, and he quiets down—finally. My shaky hands fumble with the key and lock, but I get it open and us inside at the last frantic second. Slam the door. Hear swishing tires on the wet street, and then nothing but the boyfriend erupting into another crying spell while a mean rain punches its way through the branches of the big, old weeping willow. I remove my rain jacket. Hair is soaked. When it dries it'll assume its true form: flat, thin and lifeless. I should just call out of work. "In the shed!" I order. For a moment I worry the owners will be arriving soon but then remember Forest is closed Mondays.

Co-workers know me as self-assured and tough. "I could never do what you do," Mickey says. Only with lovers am I a desperate, insecure jellyfish. My brother's respect and admiration for me, however naïve, once gave me confidence, motivated me to work harder—he has my college diploma hanging in his and Tara's bedroom. It's not enough anymore. I'm not who they think I am. I live my life alone, can barely keep a dog alive let alone sustain a human relationship. If I were successful, Pedro never would've left me. My demons wouldn't have existed or drawn me to Shoshanna's. Maybe she wouldn't be dead: the congregation of our evil friends may have exasperated our need to keep them alive. All of us suffer from a manic weakness from which the only relief, however temporary, is sharing it with one another.

"Can I have a bump, please?" He's sniveling like a kid with a boo-boo whining for a lolly.

"Yes, just stop the bellyaching."

Entering the shed I have an impulse to cross myself as if I still believed in the Catholic god. My parents forced me to learn the gesture growing up before they really fell off the deep end of their addiction to booze, coke and each other. My mother had a habit of doing the same whenever she drove drunkenly past a cemetery or church.

The shed feels like a chapel of evil, with its rusty gardening tools resting on the shelves inside like unholy instruments of sacrificial offerings. The boyfriend snatches up a pair of long, sharp-looking shears, erratically squeezing them open and closed. I hand him the bag of blow, and he drops them instantly. In a span of two seconds he's dumped on his hand every granule of cocaine and sucked it up his nose, which sounds painfully congested. The off-white powder, browning blood and clear, thick snot smeared over the lower half of his face looks like makeup for an unfamiliar Halloween costume. He's pacing back and forth, beginning sentences he can't finish, but he wants to talk, tell me *something*. Thick, drug-loaded sweat dripping from his gray beard looks like L.A. Looks hair gel. I imagine catching a dollop and styling my rain-limped locks.

"So what did you do rest of the night," he asks with obvious effort to change the subject to normal conversation—coke must be kicking in.

"Nothing... just went back to mine with Pedro for a bit."

"A bit?" he chuckles, making my blood simmer. Party people know each other too well.

"Yeah, well, had to cut it shorter than I hoped... have work today." *Pedro fainting. The corner of the kitchen table, then instant silence, and I did nothing to help him.* "...I should go."

"Don't, please!" He grabs me by the shoulders, pulls me to his chest. Sobbing ensues... I don't know who it's coming from. Our faces are dripping rain or tears or both. It doesn't matter which. My best friend is dead and so is the boyfriend's—whether or not Pedro's still breathing back at my apartment, he's dead to me. The fact that we're almost strangers to each other, my fear, disgust and hatred of him—all of it's meaningless now. We're alone, tired, desperate for something to hold onto, however brief. Rain beats the roof: the real world breaking into our brief escape from what we've done.

In this moment he's so warm: his body heat, the jittery heart pumping blood through the cut in his chin, dripping it onto my forehead, is a lie, but it's warm. I just need to feel someone again. He clearly does, too. Dip head, open mouth, invite his tongue inside. He grabs me by the hair, directing me to my knees, whips a wrinkly half-hard cock from his vomit-covered trousers and shoves it down my throat. I inhale greedily, encouraging it to full form.

This is the shed, and those are the demons crawling out of the walls like the evil, groaning shadows in *Ghost* forcibly escorting recently deceased sinners to hell. Against my knees I feel his big boots shrinking to size nine—my mother's worn white Keds. I'm positive, no need for visual confirmation—his flicking toes have become much smaller. From the corner of my left eye lies a man's arm in flannel, a smoking gun still in hand. The boyfriend thrusts deeper and faster, the damp, saw-dusted hardwood floor becoming the blood-puddled linoleum in my parents' kitchen. Caterwauling demons are on every side, their rank breath burning my cheeks, their translucent forms becoming dark and then opaque. As Shoshanna's lover-slash-murderer nears completion, they encircle us, creating the eye of a horrible tornado. He shoots a nasty load into my mouth. In parallel, the demons invade me via my stuffy ears, nose, watering eyes, and then speed down the back of my black jeans and up my asshole. Instant silence inside and outside. The downpour of rain no more. Whimpering, he pulls out, brings a veiny, dry hand to his chin. Trying not to gag as I swallow his results, I sit back on my heels, feeling the wetness in my crotch: I must've come, too.

"What just happened?"

His question merits no response. Can't speak right now, anyway. My anxiety python emerges from under my right shoe, slowly making its way round my torso: that familiar tightening...

The side door to the shed slams shut behind the boyfriend. Never saw him zip up and leave. He didn't say goodbye, but it's probably for the best. The floor returns to its original form. I stay slumped and seated on my heels, physically and mentally drained. Alone in this dark wooden box that reeks of manure, rusty tools and the boyfriend's filthy cock, I am completely present, my head utterly clear, as if I've woken from the best sleep in my life. Sunlight infiltrates cracks in the roof. I may be hearing a bird chirping a happy tune somewhere nearby.

NICO HAD BEEN in Milan for Fashion Week, Pedro and I back in New York at one of his theme parties, the name of which escapes me. He was only one beer and two MDMA capsules in when he noticed the symptoms: bloody urine that felt like glass passing through his dick hole. He was in so much pain, couldn't stand upright, was bent over like a much older man—young as he usually looked. That night he seemed ten years his senior, fear in his eyes like a born-again death-row convict on the chair believing he was about to meet his maker, realizing all the terrible things he'd done and suddenly remorseful. Pedro on shrooms, only this time with physical evidence supporting his self-destruction.

"Oh god something's really wrong," he moaned, head on my thighs in the cab to the emergency room.

After we reached Beth Israel Hospital, we learned he wasn't entirely wrong about what was coming down: one of his kidneys had collapsed… stress from drugs and drinking. They had to implant a stent, warned him to curb the partying or next time the damage might be irreversible.

Upon his release he retired to his apartment and didn't emerge for a month and a half, never responding to my Facebook messages and sporadic calls and texts. Nico and I would half enjoy the occasional one-on-one brunch, during which she'd make excuses for Pedro: he's still recovering, focusing on his art, blah blah blah. After all I'd done for him, I felt I deserved *some* attention! Apart from her reassurance and the posts of Pedro's latest artworks on Instagram, I was completely shut out.

My brief times with Nico hardly made up for Pedro's and my arguably dangerous pattern of communication. I too retreated to my apartment, often calling out of work because I was too depressed to leave my bed. A sad piano song played repeatedly in my head as my dog—in dire need of a brushing—hung off the edge of my bed, so bored he may as well have been dead, the bed sheets matted with fur and ripe with sweat from my unwashed body. Texts from Mickey came and went, along with random invitations from friends to a show or dinner, or fuck friends sent cock pics. I ignored all of them.

At night I'd dream Pedro and I were in Berlin on May Day, our arms draped across each other's shoulders as we marched through Kreuzberg with the locals. Heavily armed cops perched on buildings and stationed along the sidewalks saluted us as we paraded past, while the crowd's mood bordered on insane, their alcohol-reddened faces filled with screams. I ignored my permanently drunken mother and relentlessly belligerent father as they crept among them, composing a symphonic cacophony in honor of my lovely friendship with Pedro. Every morning I'd wake up crying because I'd woken up... But to be asleep forever...

MY SINFUL PEACE is fading, its pleasant state of now interrupted by the terrible memory of an unconscious Pedro on the wood laminate floor at my apartment. I'm back in the dirty shed, my comedown and exhaustion painfully palpable. The turning of a key and the gates to Forest sliding open along their rusty track. Heart speeding, breath held, I crawl out of the shed, like a toy my parents wouldn't get me but that I couldn't let go of in the store, nor care less that my defiance was buying me a later beating.

"The fuck!" Amanda shrieks like a chicken. The newly sunny day reflecting off Shoshanna's jewelry onto her undeserving neck pierces my eyes. Still on hands and toes like a wild animal, a werewolf that would love nothing more than to bite her fucking head off. At least it's her and not the owners. Exhale and stand, force a chuckle to suggest I was pranking her.

"You scared the shit out of me."

"Gotcha!" I muster.

"Spend the night in there, crackhead?" she snickers, lighting a joint. "Not that I'm judging. I've snuck in here a few times when Shoshy and I were fighting, or when she was with her better half—think I just saw him running down the street, strangely enough."

"I didn't know you worked here."

"Yeah, well, I need the cash and they had an opening, fucking *obvi*, right? Got them to hire me last night. Perfect timing, really."

"They're not open Mondays," I say, brushing sawdust off my black jeans with the back of my hand, which is proving more difficult in the crotch area. I point to the sign on the wall next to the gate displaying the store hours.

"Cocksuckfucker!" she lets out, slapping her thigh.

"Well, good luck, I have to get going," I say, making a beeline for the exit.

"Hey wait!" she high-pitches. "Could you do me a solid? Totally okay if you can't, and I wouldn't ask if I wasn't so desperate, but—"

"I don't have any cash on me. Sorry." Not that I'd give it to her if I did.

"No worries," she says, expelling a long, dramatic breath, disappointment painted on her drawn, sallow face. She looks down at her chest, fingers the jewelry she stole from Shoshanna, eyes brightening with an evil smile. "You know what, it's okay, actually... I'll think of something."

Disgusted, I say nothing else and just head to the street, unlock bike, put ass on seat and feet to pedals, and before putting hands on the handlebars type an email to the office: *I'm sick, something I ate, heading to doctor's, back online later, call with anything urgent.* Won't pick up if they do—will blame it on the visit running over.

The many speed bumps and potholes while I'm cycling down Kent Avenue, every tarred interruption of my journey home, forces a new memory to the big screen of my mind. Flashbacks:

one second, two max, and then I'm on the road again. But each jolt is a year.

Bump: blood quickly forming under Pedro's head like a load from his cock onstage

Hole: muscles on my mother's face collapsing in slo-mo

Hole: Dad's unexpected expression of remorse at the end

Bump: Pedro sharing my hospital bed and cradling me in the crook of his skinny arm as I sob over a lost lover

Hole: Mickey at my parents' joint funeral pulling me to him and awkwardly acting like a dad

Bump: Shoshanna's boyfriend slapping my chin with those slimy balls of his...

Lightning reflects in the glass door entrance to my building as I approach. I pull my keys from my jeans in tandem with dark clouds running over the sunny sky like a drunken driver. The natural accident thundering above sets off a few car alarms. Max is probably pissing inside, on my possibly dead best friend: like most doggies he's terrified of storms.

Key, lobby, don't check mail or take stairs, just push elevator button, numbers above it lighting up: 4, 3, 2, and here comes 1 as quickly as a horny adolescent orgasming. Can't remember this piece-of-garbage elevator ever being so eager to service me. Its floor is decorated with an empty fries-scented Shake Shack bag and the sticky-looking plastic top to a soda cup. Any other day I'd be craving a double cheeseburger—it's okay to indulge as long as I follow it up with a green juice and workout. Thoughts of eating and exercising kill my appetite, especially now when they're paired with a coke comedown. Why bother nourishing the body at the End of Us, anyway? The elevator door slides open to my floor.

I HADN'T BEEN the one to let Pedro die. As it turned out, he'd put himself in a cab after a brief fainting spell at my place, and the driver had found him unresponsive in the backseat when they'd arrived at his. I temporarily blocked the memory of him waking to find himself bleeding from the head and me sleeping on his chest on the floor of my flat. Visibly disgusted, he'd shoved me away and ran out.

I couldn't breathe the weeks following his death. It wasn't a panic attack or withdrawal in the traditional sense: a normal life was suffocating me. Weekend nights were the worst because that had been when my demon friends used to visit. They would crawl out of my ears, land on my shoulders, slide down my arms and plop onto the palms of my hands, operating my fingers like puppets, sticking them in pockets, pulling out my phone and texting, shoving plastic cards in ATMs, using sawed-off straws to diddle three or four fifty-bags of bad blow and clutching thick cocks. I used to lick those fingers clean. Early mornings at Pedro's parties, the demons would ride semen down my esophagus like a Slip 'n Slide, return to my body and recover in my Mind's Eye for six days and six nights. My demons had been born the day I'd witnessed my parents' deaths at eleven, and they died with Pedro. I'd killed them all. Or at least thought I had.

Idle, alone, didn't know what to do with myself. There were infinite nanoseconds in my newly normalized existence and no one but Max to keep me company. Sure, there were those humans who could walk the line without fail: I cleaned my cave and invited them in, but all they cared about was what used to be there. Focusing on paintings of my former lives, they ignored the stuffed demons that were also mounted on the walls. There were books. I had appealed to fiction and poetry by writers who'd committed suicide, hoping they'd shed some light on my self-hating imagination. Instead they merely perpetuated my tortured-soul stereotype. There was manic online streaming, which temporarily eased my symptoms, but in the long run all the music and movies did was depress me. And there was sociopathic social network shit, which only made me feel insecure.

My demon friends were dead in Hell, but at least they were together and having fun. After killing them, I was invited to several events advertising debauchery. To attend, I'd have had to fall off the Edge of Darkness. Hangover aches and pains would've inevitably followed the parties, but I would've no longer been bored or lonely: with Pedro and Shoshanna gone I'd have renewed my friendship with the only remaining creatures who understood me. Demons never judge, and they're there to please.

PART II

NIGHTLIGHT

For Marco at the Richardson

To be alone, to be oneself, not to be driven
or violated into something which is not oneself,
surely it is better than anything.

—D. H. Lawrence, *Aaron's Rod*

THIS IS THE coldest winter I've been through in New York, and I've lived here eleven years. Despite the weather getting warmer, they keep the heat uncomfortably high in my building, but last night I left the windows open, so it's much cooler than usual. The dripping faucets in the bathroom and kitchen didn't keep me up for once, the super having repaired them yesterday morning. Save for the sporadic sound of a distant car horn or police siren, the morning's completely silent.

My third-floor apartment faces the back, overlooks a dilapidated parking garage, the roof of which reaches the second floor below me. With my back to the only windowed wall, I'm trying for a few more minutes of sleep before prepping for work, avoiding the sunlight that bleeds through the white metal blinds and the long, white fabric panels covering the glass doors to the balcony. At the end of the bed Max lifts his head, checking me out with half-open eyes. He's been up, down, excited, disappointed, for going on six hours. He always knows I'm awake by my breathing pattern, so with my insomnia he's constantly thinking it's time to piss, shit and eat, and right now I'm wishing I never adopted him.

I ignore the dog, focus on keeping my eyes shut till I drift off again, albeit lightly, a hazy dream of Jacques and me on an aimless road trip in an unfamiliar desert, playing a game of twenty questions. He's steering a faded-black Jeep with his left hand as I sit passenger side holding his right. In the backseat a frantic-eyed Max maintains a wobbly stance, not realizing he just needs to lie down for a more comfortable ride. Jacques lifts my hand to his mouth, sticks my thumb inside and bites down hard. I yank it out, flick his ear. He scolds me for hitting him while he's behind the wheel. I can hear the tires of the jeep running over dirt and pebbles on the sand-littered freeway, feel his smooth skin as he massages my sore thumb, smell him, see the hood of the car broiling in the sun, feel the AC freezing us inside. "Turn it off," I say. "I'm cold."

"ARE YOU COLD?" he'd asked with the genuine concern only a lover or a good parent can offer. Draped his brown vintage leather jacket over my shoulders when he returned from the bathroom.

"Thanks," I said. He sat back down facing me, his clear blue eyes inviting pools, continued where he'd left off about the shoot in Iceland, having to jump into icy water for a scene, but I couldn't pay attention. Something about his plain white T-shirt, the way it stretched around his perfect torso made me scared of how safe I felt. "Want to go back to my place now?" I interrupted nervously, reminding him of our original intentions for meeting that we'd discussed on Tinder.

"In a minute," he grinned, laying a hand on mine, calming me instantly. "I really like talking to you."

I smiled, tried to accept that this might not be just a fuck.

WAKING AGAIN—A neighbor slammed the door to the exit stairwell directly outside my apartment. I check the time on my iPhone: only eleven minutes have passed. Lying on my belly in bed, reaching under it for a charger. When I plug it in, it functions intermittently. I have to jiggle the loose wire, position it just right. The charger was a Christmas gift from Jacques—I'm notorious for losing them. This one is wrapped in a zebra-patterned fabric that's coming undone. I gave him bar supplies with a sphere ice mold for his beloved scotches on the rocks, but he never took them and hasn't ever been here long enough to use them.

Hope for more sleep has evaporated and headache and body pains worsened from not enough of it. It's time to get up. I cancel the iPhone's classic-sounding alarm before its scheduled attack. Max rises, stretches every which way before shaking out the restless night. Ignoring me, he jumps off the bed and walks to the glass doors I left open, sticking his nose in between the long, white fabric panels to get a whiff of the city. I sit up slowly, eventually standing and dragging my feet to the bathroom.

A shower isn't possible today, I suddenly remember: the super had to break the tiles to replace the leaky faucet and then re-tile, which takes about forty-eight hours to dry, and it's only been twenty-four. This is especially unfortunate because I forgot to wash yesterday, the overwhelming sense of dread and anxiety over this inevitable day having paralyzed me in bed all weekend. But Monday morning is here: a half-day of work and then a good-bye visit with Jacques, so it's time to be clean again, no choice in the matter.

The faucet sputters when I first turn it on. I turn it back off, take a deep breath and turn it on again. Water flows nicely this time. Lifting one leg and then the other, I maneuver my ripe body into the cold tub, kneel and sit on my heels. With cupped hands I take the slowly warming water, mix it with body wash and begin massaging it into my thighs, working my way up my chest and into the armpits, then back down to my genitals and around and under to my asshole. Shampooing proves more difficult. Through soaped eyes I keep checking to see if I'm wetting the new tiles. Luckily, I haven't.

Rinse off. Get up. Get out of the tub. Pat myself down with a towel smelling faintly of mold, drop it to the floor. Bright round bulbs over the mirrored medicine cabinet highlight the areas on my head where I'm fairly certain my hair is thinning, most notice-ably in front. I never noticed before moving here, but having gone a month without cleaning the apartment, I can count at least two dozen light-brown hairs scattered on the tiled bathroom floor, the loss of them probably from chain-smoking, stress and aging. The skin on my thirty-two-year-old face is paler than usual, the bags under my eyes puffy from oversleeping and the beginning of al-lergy season. Oh well.

Brush teeth. Pop a couple Advil, two lithium, one Zoloft, two Klonopin. Exit bathroom. In the full-length mirror hanging on the inside of the closet door, I examine my naked body, remembering what it felt like to have Jacques touch it for the first time and thereafter. Like leaves budding in the spring, flourishing in the summer and then withering till their eventual, inevitable deaths in the fall, his lust for me fading as each month passed.

Dressing is the easiest part. Black T-shirt. Black sweatshirt. Black underwear. Black ankle socks. Black jeans. Black windbreaker. Black boots. Max is as relieved to be finally taken for a walk as I am about smoking my first cigarette of the day, a habit I reignited when I met Jacques. "Everyone smokes on set, there's so much sitting around," he's rationalized more than once. He smokes constantly and hasn't been on set in weeks.

Pick up shit. Feed dog. Grab bike from balcony. Go.

DRUNK ON ONE too many Flower Power IPAs, we had clumsily fucked in my bed. Went for a second round, but he couldn't get it up again. Not that it mattered. There was Max to play with—who wasn't as interested in doing so as Jacques—Jacques's newly moving to the city to chat about, our arms to lie in and his abnormally big blue eyes to stare into for hours.

"You can sleep here."

"I would love to," he said, nuzzling his Greek nose on my chest. "But I have to do more running around tomorrow and my friend is expecting me back tonight." He'd signed the lease on his place that afternoon, but it wouldn't be vacated for another month. In the meantime, he was crashing with a production designer friend of his who lived in Bed Stuy.

"Okay," I conceded. "I have work tomorrow, anyway." Relieved he'd said no. Didn't believe our connection would surpass that evening of fucking. What was the point of an intimate night of slumber that would eventually end in disappointment when it didn't meet my fantastical expectations?

Long kiss goodbye until his Uber arrived. Back inside. Leaning against the shut door with closed eyes and a sexually pleased grin. Thought, what a sweet, beautiful man, would be so lovely to date someone like him. Knew it wasn't in the cards for me. Too much scar tissue on the heart to sustain anything with someone like him. At least I had had him for a few hours. Tripped on something walking toward the bed: it was his wallet.

MORNING RITUALS CYCLE through my mind as I bike toward the Manhattan Bridge. Gusts of fifty-two-degree wind rap against my ears like someone frantic to get inside, away from an attacker. A gut-wrenching worry I missed a step snakes up my insides: the infamous anxiety python, nesting in my esophagus this time. Struggling to remember if I locked the front door and the sliding glass door to the balcony, applied deodorant, sprayed myself with cologne, fed the dog. I pull over, hyperventilating. Sobbing follows like an erupted volcano or popped pimple, and then I'm calmer. Return to the road.

HAD LUNCHED WITH him at The Butcher's Daughter, a juice and sandwich place on Kenmare, wide-open floor-to-ceiling windows inviting inside the hot summer day. Sat at a table on the street on white metal chairs with worn wooden seats and ordered two green juices. Shared an avocado and egg salad on toast. I handed him his wallet fat with cards, cash and receipts—hadn't invaded it the night before despite my curiosity: wanted to learn his last name, where he'd shopped, how much money he carried around, but only if he was forthcoming about it. I didn't want to steal those moments from Us.

"Thanks for holding onto it for me."

"Of course." I smiled, bright-eyed. "Thanks for trusting me enough to leave it overnight. I didn't look through it."

"I wouldn't have cared if you had." He lifted a hand to my face, traced my quivering jawline with his thick pointer finger and seemed to be reading my mind, sensing the underlying ugliness of insecurity and anxiety ingrained in my skeleton without being turned off by it. "Oh, pretty one... I'm so happy to see you again. You know that, right?"

CYCLING THROUGH RED lights now, speeding to the office, passing the corner of Myrtle and Classon where he and I met during the hotter months of last year. Removed from an evening setting and higher temperatures, an inviting breeze blowing out the candles, the aroma of beer-soaked benches in the back of the bar. Oud Wood by Tom Ford on his skin, the sweet sound of car horns and summertime conversation outside the Tap House—now it's just a closed bar on a cracked-concrete corner in a chilly borough. A driver curses me for running the light as I pass that piece of sidewalk in the sprawling graveyard of our relationship. The sky opens without warning, bawling all over me. Rush to the nearest station on Classon and Lafayette.

The subway is the most detestable mode of transportation for an avid biker with anxiety problems, but it's a tradeoff for being able to work the day in damp clothes rather than soaking wet ones. Being stuffed into those filthy cars with such a hodgepodge of people coming in from the rain is like being force-fed a nasty stew of strange meats and decayed vegetables simmered in a broth of dirty bath water. It interrupts the place in my mind, the basement in my brain where I've retreated as I follow on autopilot the same route to the city I've taken for months. Now I have to interact with people, be cognizant of others, remove my backpack, apologize to those I've accidentally tapped with the grimy tires of my bike while navigating it through a packed car.

The underground station is chock full of mismatched riders—some native to the area, others who've infiltrated it over the last few gentrifying years—crammed in so tightly the toes of the shoes on those in the front of the crowd are sticking out over the track. If a train were to charge through now, they'd all be maimed. The electronic sign hanging above our impatient heads and the sing-song voice over the intercom say the next train will arrive in eleven minutes. As I tunnel through the crowd with my bike, "Excuse me, sorry, excuse me," I'm greeted with snarky looks and bitchy glances, which add to my dark mood, a festering wound—so much so I wish I could push one or two of them over the edge. They'll topple onto the tracks, get covered in filth and a cockroach in their ear, or bit by a rat or electrocuted on the third rail.

A hipster couple hanging all over each other interrupts my imagined revenge. They move aside, smiling, gesturing to a spot near the wall where I can lean my bike, inadvertently revealing a giant poster for the upcoming premiere of the final season of *One Degree*. The actress Zoe Severin caresses Jacques's handsome profile with a pale hand, his guilty eyes turned to the camera. Uneasy feelings crawl up my back like millions of baby spiders. I use my bike to force my way through the couple, separating them.

"Watch it, fuck," he says.

"What an ungrateful bitch," she says.

Ignore them. Keep going. Avoid the looks of the crowd.

Around fifteen minutes pass. No subway yet, but the voice returns: "The train is being detained at Myrtle because of a sick passenger." My guess is it's another morning suicide. The voice recommends a nearby bus line. Outside again, and the rain's stopped.

A DOWNPOUR THAT first weekend. We had locked ourselves inside with two hangovers, Netflix and three food deliveries via seamless.com evenly punctuating the day. Had done blow together for the first time the night before. Not sure if it was just the comedown, but every drama we saw made him cry, and me subsequently—especially *Sophie's Choice*. I'd never had a grown man sob in front of me, would've usually turned me off but not with him. Manically compulsive sex continued throughout the weekend. We attempted to rise on Sunday, spent less than thirty minutes at the gym before returning to our home in my bed: "The Bubble" is what we called it.

The Bubble continued. Took the following week off work; "an impromptu holiday," I informed my boss. Over dinner one night I confided in Jacques about my familial past—the violent deaths of my parents, my history of mental illness, which he took in stride after a deep breath or two. "I'm well now," I promised. He did the same with stories of the crazy ex-girlfriend he left because she wanted kids and grew increasingly jealous the longer they'd been together, and told me he'd been hospitalized at fourteen and put on suicide watch for a few weeks. He said the end of his parents' marriage and the beginning of puberty had instigated the breakdown, but he'd had the darkness in him for as long as he could remember. He did grow out of it, becoming the happy, healthy, non-medicated, demonless adult he is today.

He claimed the move to New York wasn't an escape from his ex but a way to audition for roles since nothing was happening in Los Angeles at the time and his agent was based in Manhattan. Easier to go to meetings in person than emailing videos made on his iPhone. He ended up doing the same for opportunities in LA, which seemed to come much more regularly than potential New York parts. I'd begun helping him audition by feeding him the other lines and holding the camera. "Read flatly, don't try to act, it's distracting," he'd often reprimand, which didn't bother me at all and produced a lovely warm feeling. After all, he was trusting me enough to let me help him further his stardom, which he held dearer than anything—or anyone—else.

BIKE LANE ON Chrystie is busier now that spring is coming. Don't remember cycling over the Manhattan Bridge but have luckily snapped out of it in time to stop at the light and prepare for the creepy cop hiding behind a parked car, waiting to ticket whichever one of us cyclists runs a red. The light turns green. Continue onward, ready to glare nastily when I spot her. When I do, she's between two cars, writing up an unfortunate someone she has already caught.

"On your right. Move over," says a bearded biker behind me farther down the path.

I don't move, keep cycling, now at below-average speed.

"On your right."

I ignore him, go slower.

"On your fucking right!" he screams. His hostility awakens in me a familiar, uncontrollable violence—possibly a genetic one—like the rising full moon that brings out a monster. Coming to an abrupt halt, I force him to do the same.

"Fuck you, you ugly motherfucker. Fuck you!" Stunned by my reaction, he falls on his side, his unprotected head and elbow smacking the street in tandem, the sound of the impact reminding me of a heavy hardcover book hitting the ground. He tries pulling himself to his feet as if nothing happened, but his shaking legs give in and he falls on his ass. "I hope you get hit by a fucking car next time," I say quietly.

He says nothing, stays down like road kill, wincing in pain. A concerned group of power-walking Asian ladies are hurrying over to make sure he's okay. I cycle around them, getting a hundred or so feet away before having to stop at the light on a traffic-packed Delancey. I look back just as they're helping him up, while he's offering me his middle finger. Way back I spot the cop, so as soon as the light turns green I'm turning right, left, right, my heart beating, hands shaking. Wracked with a sudden onslaught of guilt, I just keep thinking: I wanted to hurt him so badly.

A SECOND WEEK of Jacques and me dating had followed the first. I returned to work, and he remained at my place, made dinner every night, introduced me to different kinds of wine—all of which I've forgotten.

"You may as well get your things and stay here till your place is ready," I said casually.

"I'm just worried we're jumping a step, you know?" he said. "Missing out on the romance in the beginning. Things should be happening more gradually."

"We have plenty of romance already, don't we? Anyway, you're here all the time... Don't worry, it doesn't mean we're committed to each other. And if it gets weird, you can leave. No expectations."

"Pretty one... I don't know."

After I offered two or three more times over the next two or three days, he finally accepted.

AT THE OFFICES of Hustle Advertising, I'm an evil zombie speaking in monotone as I give the creatives more shit than usual for late work, nitpicking the language in scope-of-work contracts proposed by third-party vendors; instructing Rosemarie, the account director on Scent-Ease—the air freshener brand I also work on—to schedule her own briefings when I usually just acquiesce. "You do realize the role of a producer is not synonymous with that of a personal assistant, right?"

I get a text from my boss, Fung Chung, Director of Production: *I need to see you now. Meet me in the birdcage on 2.* She's always in meetings, never available, rarely responds to emails and runs the department like a sweatshop. Once executive producer at White Advertising, she left for the Hustle gig and took me with her, promoting me to senior producer on Scent-Ease and giving me double the pay I'd been making.

I've been told the osprey is Hustle's mascot because of its unique behavior in hunting and catching prey, i.e., Hustle's specialization in snagging unsuspecting consumers with manipulative advertising for their massive portfolio of automotive, luxury and beauty brands, which is why there's a giant birdcage for a conference room on every level of the building. Fung is in the gilded pen on the second floor, sitting on the swing, left hand clutching one of the two ropes from which the seat is hung while texting with her right. Her hair is in two side buns, she has a chubby upper body and bird legs. Today—as she has every day this month in a variety of wild patterns and colors—she's wearing a fuzzy sweater, pleated miniskirt, tights and tennis shoes.

"Hey, Fung," I say flatly.

"Have a seat," she says, pointing with a pinky to the feathery yellow couch in the back of the cage. When I sit, my eyes are in line with the toes of her black-and-white-checkered tennis shoes. She puts the phone on her lap and goes for a swing, her legs flying above my head, the whoosh of air shifting my hair. "How's it going on Scent-Ease? We haven't met in a while."

"I know… I asked if you had five minutes on Monday, and you told me you were booked until the week after next, so I sent you an invite to catch up then…"

Silence.

"It's fine," I continue, "I mean they're asking us to produce an interactive video that ties into their scratch-and-sniff print campaign, where you can actually smell the scents while choosing your own adventure in the video, but I told them the technology's just not there yet, so—"

"That's not exactly true. Maybe it's not possible on dot-com or mobile, but what about an experiential event? How about 'smelling booths' outside the Flatiron with touch panels and auto-initiated sprays? We can work with that vendor Punchy. They do that sort of thing."

"Yeah, experiential, yeah, but they wanted a solve for digital."

"Look. You need to approach your work more creatively. That's what a *senior* producer does. It's why I hired you." She indiscreetly sticks a hand up her skirt, her nails scratching the abrasive-looking pink tights underneath. It makes me think of the Scent-Ease ads and wonder if she'll sniff afterward. Pulling out, she tugs around the inner right thigh, seeming to have freed a wedgie.

The left side of her head is still a bit concave but nothing compared to last year. Her plastic surgeon has since filled it with fat from her ass—twice. In her hospital bed she demanded—albeit weakly—that I bring her work phone, acting as if she hadn't just suffered a massive brain aneurysm two weeks before. She had a patchy buzz cut adorning roughly half of her round head, the rest sprouting those familiar straight black locks, which were limp and greasy. A good chunk of her skull was sitting on ice till the swelling in her brain subsided. Her head looked like the infamous Tom Brady deflated football, was something out of a gory science fiction film I could only bear to sit through once. Likewise, my visiting her was limited to the one time. Some might say she's a tough woman with an unwavering work ethic, but her self-induced stress from the job, poor diet and nightly drinking is what nearly killed her—and she's only in her early thirties. And now, nearly a year later, she's right back to working like a maniac. Looking away, I'm hoping she didn't notice me checking out her deformity.

Having sympathy for her at the time was difficult. I just kept remembering when I came in my first day horribly sick with strep throat and a hundred-and-three-degree fever—I'd known Jacques had had it and would give it to me, didn't care, couldn't stay away; after I nursed him back to health he left for a shoot, leaving me sick and alone—had been in so much pain I could barely swallow my saliva. Perspiring with infection, I'd waited in the reception area nearly two hours before she showed up, brought me to this very birdcage: "Here's the org chart, here's the Scent-Ease master service agreement and project roadmap. It's a four-million-dollar piece of business. Don't fuck it up," she said. "You look like shit by the way." No details on the status of the current project work, no intros to the account or creative teams, no concern for my health let alone permission to go home and recover.

"Okay," I say presently, "but it's not what they asked for in the brief. I'll bring it up with Account, but I doubt they'll go for it."

"Great," she replies, her wide nose in her iPhone. "Fuck, I'm late for a meeting." She hops off the swing, almost kicking me in the face. "Oh. The reason I wanted to meet is I've been getting complaints about your communication style."

"You mean Rosemarie? She's treating me like her assistant again and I called her out on it. That's all. She's not my boss."

"She's not, but she's still a director and above you, so you need to watch it with her. Just work it out. I won't feel like defending you again. Shit, I gotta go."

THE BUBBLE HAD been on the brink of bursting as Jacques's and my first weeks together wore on. His apartment wouldn't be ready for three more weeks than he'd originally been told. Concurrently he'd been turned down for a couple of big parts, whose audition scenes I'd recorded with him. In one, an action-thriller, his character was the hot younger brother of Gerard Butler; in the other, a pill-addicted genius hacker confronting an online child pornographer. I began to worry that he resented me for his not getting cast. We'd been hung over when we recorded both auditions, the behind-the-scenes featuring him scolding me for either overacting or not giving him enough. Portraying a brute and creepy molester proved out of my range.

I'd come home from work each night, and he'd be frantically emailing business contacts or on the phone with his agent, manager or publicist, having a Skype meeting with a director or producer, learning lines for more auditions, or already drunk on expensive wine. Online ordering of food deliveries cancelled out the nightly homemade meals. Sometimes eating was altogether replaced by generous helpings of booze and blow. It had been the longest he'd ever been out of work. In the back of my mind was a constant feeling of worry about the possibility that I was a nasty bad-luck charm, responsible for his extended dry spell, and for good reason.

Before we'd met I'd been excruciatingly lonely, was in some of my darkest days, had lost my best friend Pedro to a bad head injury following a night of hard partying together. PEDRO FOREVER graffiti infected the five boroughs, on billboards, store windows, subway walls, city streets and sidewalks. It'd become more of a fad than an artistic tribute to my dead friend and only served as constant fuel for my grief, not to mention that of his surviving girlfriend Nico, who'd blamed me for his death and hasn't spoken to me since. Recurring nightmares of my parents' deaths—and my childhood life with them—were at their highest since my teen years. While meeting Jacques dissolved some suffering, I couldn't help thinking it was partially because he'd absorbed my pain. Guilt was growing on my brain like a cauliflower wart. As much as I'd have hated for him to leave me for months on a shoot, I believed I could've sacrificed The Bubble to relieve his despair the way he had mine.

One night I arrived home and he was coming from the bathroom all smiles, cleanly shaven for an in-person audition to play the lead on a new show on USA. Movies were the ultimate goal, but he'd become a bit desperate for anything to settle the ambition boiling in his blood—something I understood quite well. He was beyond excited, kissed me literally head to toe when I walked inside. Whatever I wanted to eat, do, was on him.

"This is it, pretty one! I feel it."

"I can, too!" I exclaimed, as thrilled as he was. Took a quick piss in the bathroom, saw the hair he had shaved all over the sink and came out half-heartedly giving him a hard time for not cleaning up after himself. His manically happy mood instantly shifted to fury.

"Fuck you! Fuck you! This is why I don't want to live here. What the fuck am I *doing* here with you? You make me move in and then bitch me out over some bullshit!"

Heart plummeting to knees. "What? Jacques, I was only joking. I thought you were in a great mood. What is this?" Moved toward him, touched his shoulder. He smacked it away and shoved me to the ground.

"I was until you fucking came home!" He threw on some clothes and left me tearing up on the floor, completely confused.

He didn't return until after 2AM, had turned off his phone. I'd downed a couple of Klonopin to calm myself to sleep. Drunk and sobbing, he shook me awake. He was so sorry. How could he be so cruel to his pretty one? We made sloppy love, both of us virtually incoherent. That was the night of our first big fight and the night I fell in love with him. Learning he was less in control than he'd initially let on, that the demons he'd supposedly vanquished as a teenager were alive and well, just better hidden than mine, I knew we were meant to be together forever.

AT BED BATH & Beyond I'm buying two Mrs. Meyer's Clean Day scented candles in lemon verbena and lavender, killing time until I meet Jacques for our last day together before he moves. They're cheaper here than they are at the corner deli on the Lower East Side where I usually get them. As the cashier rings me up, I'm remembering Jacques saying at dinner Friday that the restaurant had the same brand in their bathroom, that they wouldn't buy expensive candles just to neutralize toilet odors. A woman sitting next to us interrupted our conversation to compliment him on his Chanel eyeglasses, said he looked familiar. Soon after she was using a selfie stick on him and half the bar was asking to be photographed with him, while he played to cliché perfection the gracious celebrity, knowing too well how to humble his strikingly pale blue eyes.

I've always looked down upon those who idolize "stars," shamelessly hunting them on the street like deer, hoping to shoot one with their iPhone for a trophy they can hang on the social networks of drank-the-Kool-Aid counterparts who are as desperate for digital attention as they are, and equally jealous when others outnumber them in "likes" and "friend" requests. Sure, I've been proud of my boyfriend's successful career—an extremely rare achievement in his profession—but the public celebration of it has only made our relationship more complicated.

A dictatorial text from Jacques: *Here. Meet me outside now.* Hastily pay for my wares. Cashier offers a bag, but I hurriedly stuff the candles in my black backpack like a first-time shoplifter, rushing out before the receipt is printed. A large-framed female security guard ignores my exit.

Nearing Jacques, I sense the anxiety python choking my stomach like a corset: the unsettling feeling of getting what I want, if only temporarily: him. It's always been him and always will be long after he's left me for good—I know that much. All those times I stood in front of my building staring longingly down the street like a hungry dog leashed outside a restaurant, waiting for my owner to arrive from the airport, an audition, a business dinner or movie premiere; the countless occasions I lay in bed on coke hallucinating his figure on the balcony because he'd come home from a shoot earlier than planned and scaled the building to surprise me.

He hasn't looked up from his phone yet, and I'm hoping he doesn't before I'm directly in front of him. Merely the thought of him watching me as I approach almost sets off a panic attack. When I'm finally close enough to be received comfortably, his phone rings. His disguise today is composed of his Chanel's over his TV-star eyes and his thick, dark hair hidden under the black beanie I bought him for his birthday. Then he sees me, one-arm-hugs me, kisses me discreetly—on the cheek—mouths "sorry" before walking away to chat with his agent or manager.

Worried my breath smells from chain-smoking, I shove a shaky hand into my backpack, feeling around for a rock-hard piece of gum stuck inside the sleeve of a production book from the last Scent-Ease shoot. Bite down on the stale stick, chewing quickly before he returns with a furrowed brow and disturbed upper lip.

"Sorry," he says sourly. "Think I'm gonna fire my manager."

"Why," I ask, uninflected. Knowing our relationship is about to end, I'm lacking the energy to feign concern.

"Nothing, he just wants me to audition for a male version of *Revenge*. I don't know how many times I have to tell him I don't want to sign a seven-year contract for some shitty TV show. I want to do *movies*."

"You will. It's only a matter of time. It's a numbers game," I say robotically, trying to remember how many times I've had this conversation with him. He's back to his phone, texting manically.

"No, I know… I'm just so sick of the back and forth."

"Well," I say, taking a breath, "would it hurt to work on a show and then do movies in between?"

"Forget it. I shouldn't be talking to you about work, anyway. You don't understand."

Spit out gum, light a cigarette. "Okay… How was the meeting with the producer?"

"Fine. Whatever. Do you want some of this?" He hands me a white plastic bag. "It's chicken teriyaki from my meeting with the producer. *I know* we're supposed to have lunch, but I couldn't say no to her."

"It's okay. No, I'll wait." Now that we're past initial greetings, my nerves seem to have calmed a bit. We walk toward my locked-up bike. As I'm removing the U-lock from the bike rack, I glance up to him frowning and teary-eyed.

"Pretty one… I'm gonna miss you."

"Stop," I say. "No sad stuff now. I can't take it. Can we please at least *try* to enjoy the day?"

"Okay… but when can we cry?" I used to find his mawkishness endearing. Now all it does is make me wonder how deeply he feels about me. But then he pulls me close, hugging me with both arms.

"Later. Please, Jacques." Tears want to come, but I pull away just in time. "What should we do today?" He's texting on his phone again, giggling.

"The producer I met at lunch was so awesome. She says the movie is still happening, just not till the end of summer."

"This is the modern Frankenstein one?"

"Yeah, she kept recommending all these places to eat in Brooklyn. I didn't have the heart to tell her I was moving to Los Angeles in the morning." The sun is gone. The gray light of an overcast sky bears down on us as we walk aimlessly down Sixth Avenue, speckles of water tapping my face intermittently, becoming visible on my jacket. "Holy shit. Look up," he says, pointing a finger at a penthouse apartment on the corner of Twelfth and Sixth. A mass of water is pouring off the balcony, cascading down the building. Pedestrians in all directions are stopping to stare at the spectacle. I'm envisioning a lonely socialite dead in an overflowing bathtub, having drowned after an overdose of pills knocked her out—she probably slit her wrists first but not deep enough to bleed out.

Continuing down the avenue, we near IFC to check out what's playing, settling on *White God*, a Hungarian film about killer dogs. The next showing isn't for another hour, so I lock my bike outside the theater. We walk toward SoHo in silence, a wedding veil of rain draping our heads. Stopped on the corner of Houston and Sixth, we watch the traffic rumbling by on the potholed streets. He removes his eyeglasses, uses my sweatshirt to clean them. I pull the hood of my black windbreaker over my head. Light turns red, cars stop. I start to move but he pulls me into a bear hug once again.

"I need to know you're going to be okay. Please tell me, pretty one. You really scared me when we talked last week."

I could say I'll be fine, ease his worry and feelings of guilt for leaving me, for giving up on New York and me and running back to LA, but I can't say the words. Holding over him the threat of hurting myself is the only leverage I have left.

"Are you really flying out in the morning?"

"I said I was," he answers, pulling away.

"I know, but you also said you bought your ticket for Sunday night when we were arguing, and you didn't really."

"Look, I'm really leaving tomorrow. My flight's in the morning at 11:15."

"Alright."

We turn onto Greene. He's relating his plans to stop home in Montreal for Easter—big holiday in Canada, I'm told—then fly back to L.A. with his father, who'll be visiting his new place for a week. The thought of Jacques starting anew on the other side of the country less than a year after I helped him make a home here makes my body ache. All those days I took off from work to be at his apartment accepting furniture deliveries from Design Within Reach and West Elm and BoConcept, while he was off shooting retakes and partying in Budapest; or helping him record additional dialogue for a film in Canada on my birthday; or those two months in France in the fall when he disappeared to make that movie; the weekends I went looking for vintage lamps at Brooklyn Flea on Lafayette Avenue and in Williamsburg; and waiting for Time Warner Cable to wire his apartment for internet access and National Grid to turn on the gas because he never got around to calling them when he moved in—it's all been for naught. I never really wanted anything in return. I don't know what I wanted. His love, I guess.

We near BoConcept where he spots a sign advertising a series of short films playing in the store to promote their products, one of which is starring the Danish girl with whom he worked on the French movie. She's posing with an older man, a well-known actor who's been in films I've enjoyed but will never be able to watch again because they'll remind me of this moment—as will most parts of Brooklyn and Manhattan and movies on Netflix. She's lying on a mauve microfiber couch by BoConcept with her legs draped over his, a dribble of blood at the corner of her mouth. He's sitting straight, staring blankly into the camera. Jacques insists we go in to watch.

"Excuse me," he says with a charismatic voice that demands attention, "are you screening the short shown on the poster outside?"

A bit embarrassed that he's asking a salesman to help us see a long-form commercial rather than expressing interest in making a purchase, I distance myself, pretending to be browsing the minimalist furniture, a few of the pieces he already has from ordering online.

"Certainly!" says a chipper white guy. Wearing a tight, white button-down shirt and a brown tie that looks like it's choking him, he guides Jacques to a desktop computer at the back of the store. My initial concern over the situation dissipates, so I join them just as the salesman is pulling up the eleven-minute video on YouTube.

"This one, yes?"

"Yeah, the girl is a friend of mine."

"Oh really?" asks another salesman popping into view. Middle Eastern, he's dressed more casually in a horizontally striped T-shirt. "How so?"

"We did a movie together."

"Oh great, which one?"

"Shush, Andy," says the other with a wink, "they want to watch."

The video plays: a sappy story about a vampire breaking up with her lover in an ultramodern apartment filled top to bottom with BoConcept furniture, lighting and decorations, the Tame Impala song "Feels Like We Only Go Backwards" as soundtrack. We hover over the computer in silence.

I begin to space out as Jacques giggles at his friend's acting, reminding me of the first time I saw him in *One Degree*. couldn't bring myself to watch it at the beginning of our relationship. Seeing my lover act made me feel horribly uncomfortable. But it seemed to hurt him that I'd never seen the show or the few films he'd been in, so I decided to do so while he was away shooting something new. Thought it might help alleviate the weight of missing him, which I carried in my belly like an unwanted baby. Instead it grew heavier. The incestuous intimacy he shared with his on-screen sister, knowing he had had a relationship with her in real life, observing his moves making fake love, recognizing some, others seeming alien, the way he laughed and got angry, I felt like I didn't know him at all. By the time I graduated to the second season of the show, my mind's resistance went from uncomfortable to unbearable. I stopped watching.

Five minutes into the short, his attention has shifted to texting. The Middle Eastern has gone over to assist a newly arrived customer, and the chipper white one is getting fidgety.

"Thanks, that's enough," Jacques says. "Now that I know it's on YouTube I can just watch the rest later."

"Yes, all links are on the website." He closes the browser window. "Would you like to check out some of the furniture in the film?"

Jacques's phone rings. "I have to take this. Thanks again, man!" he says, rushing to the exit.

"We actually bought furniture from your online shop a few months ago," I say.

"Oh. How lovely."

"Thanks again."

Outside, Jacques on the phone, weaving around the rusty foundation of the scaffolding above. "But I *need* it all here by next week. I can pay extra... It can't wait another week. I have family visiting the first day I move in... What's that?... Yes, that's fine. I'll call my accountant after this and have it wired... Thanks so much, man, really appreciate it."

I'm picturing the white owl lamp from West Elm that I bought him as a housewarming gift sitting on a new shelf in his new loft in Downtown LA. He's stumbling through the front door with some famous actor or actress, drunk and high on blow. Reaching for the switch on the lamp, he turns it on, at the same time knocking it off the shelf. It smashes onto the floor, reduced to glossy ceramic fragments. He and his lover cackle, blow lines on the industrial-style coffee table and fuck messily on the gray microfiber couch that I waited hours to be delivered to his apartment here, staining it with sweat and come.

He squeezes my shoulder. "You okay, pretty one?" I take a deep breath, open the drain behind my eyes, give him a tight-lipped smile.

"Yes. Where to next?"

Violent rain falls abruptly. Without umbrellas, we walk only as far as the scaffolding stretches. On the way, we spot a gallery displaying works by a painter named Sam Wolfe Connelly and decide to go in. Two male gallerists barely look up to nod as we enter, quickly returning to their chitchat about so-and-so's hot new boyfriend. Jacques circles the room speedily, spending no time studying the work. "Not really my style," he says.

A painting named *Away Team* has a strong effect on me. In it a man is lying on his back on a dirty mattress, his head and torso concealed under a dark blanket, his legs sticking out, wearing classic black Nikes with a white swoosh on the side. A large knife to the right of the mattress lies parallel with the body, but there's no blood. Two possibilities: he stabbed himself before covering up with the blanket, the mattress absorbing the blood, or murdered someone and is feeling guilty about it, as if hiding under a blanket will grant him asylum from the hellish world he made for himself. It could be both, that he murdered someone and then killed himself.

"I want this one. I want to hang it over my bed. It's so cool." Jacques walks over to evaluate my selection.

"Um, absolutely not. You? Thank god you can't afford it."

With a swipe of my last working credit card, I pay for the painting at the front of the gallery. He shakes his head in disapproval. The gallerists have gone from ignoring us to doting on me. I arrange the delivery of the painting for Thursday of next week, and then leave.

The rain has tapered off, enough for us to venture past the scaffolding. We pop into a café so he can take a shit in the customers-only bathroom. I pretend to be mulling over the menu hanging above the sandwich display case, not that anyone's watching. Real customers are paying at the register, *tourist* written all over their attire. They ask questions in broken English, the impatient cashier responding loudly like they're deaf. Two children are tinkering with Pez dispensers shaped like characters from *Frozen*. The sound of the crinkling of the plastic packaging feeds my chronic unease. One of the sandwich makers behind the counter is wiping his nose with a rubber-gloved hand before getting back to work. If I were ordering when I observed this, I wonder if I would have asked him to re-glove.

On the walk back to the theater, Jacques is going on about his new loft in Downtown LA, showing off photos, comparing the size and look of it to those here in SoHo. I can see the similarities between the two, but he discounts the dramatic difference in location: of course an apartment in a soulless industry town is going to be cheaper and almost as nice.

He orders popcorn at the movies with no butter. "Just a Diet Coke for me," I say, immediately thereafter drowning out his bitching about how aspartame will be the death of me. The movie, which takes place in Budapest, is like an adult version of *Homeward Bound*. Every five to fifteen minutes, he makes a comment: "I've been there," "We shot on that bridge," "I'm friends with that dude who plays one of the dogcatchers." He goes on to say that whenever they shoot bigger budget films there they hire the locals. Sometimes they act, and at other times they work as the gaffer or props master or production assistant—apparently the guy playing the dogcatcher has done all four.

Toward the end of the film, the protagonist, a canine actor whom critics are calling the Al Pacino of dogs, turns on the humans, sick of all the abuse, the movie morphing into an updated version of the '90s horror flick *Man's Best Friend*. As he and a pack of hundreds of other dogs flood the city, mauling everyone to death, they run into the girl who owned the lead pooch earlier in the film. Approaching her with a snarl, he and his cohorts are about to lunge at her pale, white throat. She gets out her trumpet and plays a familiar tune for him until he lies down in defeat, coiling in guilt for losing his shit, the countless dogs behind him following suit. At this moment, the credits begin rolling, as do tears from Jacques's eyes. He clutches my left bicep—discreetly, of course.

"I'm going to miss you so much, pretty one." I hear the four or five other viewers in the tiny theater rising and leaving. "Say something," he says. "You're acting so cold. Is this how you want to spend our last day together, like it's not happening?"

The burning saliva in my esophagus begins bubbling. A heat rises up my throat and through my sinuses. Saline erupts through my eyes. The two of us sob all over each other. Then I remember hearing somewhere that love isn't sentimental. If that's true, I don't know what we're doing here or why I feel so horrible.

In a porn store he's flipping through a rack of edible undies in clear packaging, telling me a story about one holiday when he and his family pulled gifts from a grab bag and his sister ended up with his contribution of strawberry-flavored panties. She found it amusing, but their mother was irate.

At the mention of his mother, of whom he speaks as if she's from an affluent French background when he's already revealed she's from a working-class family, I recall one of my last arguments with him when he told me I would never meet her, nor any of his family or any other friends:

The night before I had had a bad reaction to the blow and booze we'd been ingesting for hours and became extremely paranoid imagining he and his twenty-one-year-old prop stylist friend had gone to the bathroom to fuck. "I've never done cocaine before," she'd said in a whiny, singsong voice. "Will you come show me, Jacques?" Normally, I wouldn't have minded the blatant flirtation, but in my intoxicated state I lost it. I suppose him keeping our relationship secret further fueled my behavior, that and him saying earlier in the evening, after returning from a two-month shoot a week before, that he was having trouble being together all the time, now that it was a "real relationship" and not just some unattainable fantasy he'd dreamed about while stuck in an under-heated trailer during a shoot in Nowhere, Canada.

At Mast Books, a lovely used bookstore in the East Village, he buys me a first edition of *Last Exit to Brooklyn*. "Something to remember me by," he says, knowing it's my favorite book. In this moment it's comforting—more sentiment—but when he's gone it'll burn a hole in my nightstand and I'll never read it again.

I'll take other memories with me: New Year's Eve at the Museum of Sex until the wee hours of New Year's Day when he decided to invite an NYU student we'd found on Tinder to join us for a threesome; the stench of latex and MDMA filling our noses as we took affectionate selfies in which I'm slightly cross-eyed with sallow skin, his eyes more protruding than usual but filled with love.

Slammed doors. Broken Bulleit bottle. Clothes chucked into the hall with a nude third wheel whom he said I punched in the face, although I don't remember that part. Rather than comforting me for having a manic episode over seeing him stick his unwrapped cock inside a stranger when we'd agreed no fucking, he asked me if he needed to be concerned for his safety, was I going to murder him like my father had my mother—granted he was high on coke when he said it. He'd never been more embarrassed in his entire life and *I* needed to hold *him*, convince him that everything was okay. Maybe this is a bad example.

Thanksgiving at my brother Mickey's in Bridgeport. I had had to beg Jacques to attend. He's chummy with the socialite Kelsey Lippman, daughter of eighties rock legend Bite; and she clearly wants his cock based on the text messages I've seen her send while I'm looking over his shoulder in bed. "But Kelsey's a good friend, and she invited me to Bite's house for Thanksgiving. I mean, c'mon, it's *Bite*," he said, toying with me before finally agreeing to come. My brother Mickey's over-emotional, pregnant girlfriend Tara gushing to her god about everything she's thankful for: her female fetus, my brother and the fact that I've finally found someone to "share the rest of my life with." I could've died, and Jacques turned about as red as I could feel myself doing. During the rest of dinner I told bland stories about a movie he and I had seen, zip-lining upstate a couple weeks before, joint trips to the gym. He'd nod with clenched teeth. Outside for a smoke, while Mickey napped and Tara did the dishes, Jacques scolded me for repeatedly saying "we." He hates those who say it because it implies each has no singular identity. Dessert was okay, and the Zip-Car drive back to Brooklyn with him and Max involved intimate conversation. That's better.

Better than now, in my apartment, when he's punching me in the arm, telling me to shut the fuck up, that I don't know anything.

"And don't think I didn't notice you've been ordering delivery online with my card... Did you ever even wire me back the money I loaned you to move in here?"

"Yes," I lie, but he'll never know. By the time he speaks with his accountant, he'll be too far up the ass of a potential "game-changer" role to remember which day of the week it is, let alone this moment. "And I bought our delivery tonight and dinner the other night, so what does it matter?" I add. "What are you so angry about? Because I don't want to watch *Family Guy*?"

He growls loudly. "Ugh, you don't get it! You never do. It's not that you don't want to watch *Family Guy*. You just don't want to watch this episode because it parodies the Tea Party and you know shit about it. I'm Canadian and I know more about U.S. politics than you ever will! And what's worse, you don't care!" He paces the room, running the palms of his hands over his greasy hair—having taken a tip from his stylist on the set of the French film, he's been washing it once a week, and conditioning it with coconut oil the rest of the week.

"What does it matter if I care about politics or not! You've never read most of the books I have. God, you act like I'm dumb."

"That's what you sound like!" He pulls on his underwear. "I don't even know why I felt sorry for you enough to say goodbye in person." Tiny needles attack my inner arms, the soles of my feet. His words are reverse acupuncture, inducing anxiety rather than alleviating it.

"Fuck you, Jacques. Did it ever occur to you that you feign concern for world issues because you're a vapid actor? I think it's pretty clear who the superficial one is. You act as if you're about to become this big movie star when all you're really doing is riding the coattails of a cancelled HBO series." This is when he punches me in the shoulder, aware it's the one with the partially torn rotator cuff from an old bicycle injury, and pushes me to the floor.

"This is over. This has been over. You think you love me and that this is some sad ending to a beautiful relationship! Pfft. You don't know the *first thing* about love. Love is a communion. I've been in love, and I will be again, and you're going to be here alone forever. Fucking vampire, that's all you are. Glenn Close in *Fatal Attraction*. Fucking scary."

"Oh, I'm the crazy one? What about your insane mood swings, sobbing one minute, screaming and hitting me the next, then suddenly happy? Why is it okay for you to treat me like that but I have to act like I'm perfect or else?"

"Because I don't love you!" he blurts out. "Don't you get it by now? Why do you make me say it? God, you're so damaged." Max is doing the Shiba Inu scream while running in circles behind me. Jacques is fastening the laces of his tennis shoes when I jump to my feet and sock him in the back. Tears of frustration begin flowing.

"Why are you even here! Why did you come if this is what you think of me?" Max is barking from the bathroom now, his safe place. "Look what you're doing to the dog! You're scaring the dog!" He picks up his T-shirt from the floor, his last article of clothing.

"You really want me to leave?" he asks, sounding slightly winded from the assault. "You're kicking me out when you know I have someone subletting my place?"

I sink into my bed, hugging my pillow, feeling sick from the melodramatic scene we're making yet unable to escape it. And I'm not sure I want to. I'm realizing now: we've been feeding off each other's weaknesses since we met. This is why we're together: my desperate, obsessive need to be loved and his to feel worshipped.

The buzzer goes off. Max erupts into a bark, having morphed from a pussy to a wolf at the sound of a bell. Jacques speaks into the intercom, pushes the button. The food is here. We ordered from our favorite guilty-pleasure place: a milkshake shop that also sells cheeseburgers.

Gradually taking in my surroundings again, I stare with watery vision at the wall, at one of his old coke-boogers encrusted on it, remembering I haven't cleaned in over a month. I feel him looking down at me as he sighs heavily. Through the dog's serious howls, I faintly hear the elevator ding, someone dragging their feet down the hall, the crinkling of a plastic bag and finally a hard knock. He opens the door.

"Hey man, thanks. Do I need to sign?"

"Nah."

"Okay, thanks."

The door closes. I hear him walking into the kitchen, opening a cabinet, pulling out a couple of plates and setting them on the table.

"I hope you have ketchup 'cause you know they always forget."

I take a deep breath. "Yeah, there's some somewhere. Behind the milk, I think."

I hear him rummaging through the fridge, exhaling in frustration. "I can't find it. Can you just come get it?"

Rising, I wipe my eyes and turn to him, a compulsive smile spreading across my face.

"Oh, you think this is so fucking funny, don't you."

"No."

"Come on, let's just eat."

THE MINUTE MY eyes shut The Eyeballs infiltrate an infinitely black space, thousands of them, in a variety of sizes, directing their attention at me, an ocular army ready to attack. They stare silently, unblinkingly, save for the sudden opening and shutting of a single lid, a rogue soldier greedy for lubrication, praying the others won't notice even though they do. Without averting their gaze, they move tightly together, surrounding the offender. An unsettling squishy sound grows louder and louder till the guilty one pops like a fat zit on the face of a thirteen-year-old. Chunky, milky insides tinged with blood pour down The Eyeball Wall. To avoid being blinded by the mess, its former counterparts are permitted to close themselves momentarily but must quickly reopen after it passes or face the same fate. For years this awful nightmare has been feeding my trypophobia—vomit-inducing disgust for and skin-crawling fear of irregularly clustered holes—usually brought on by extreme stress.

A thunderstorm over my bed interrupts the night terror. There's no rain, just jarring sounds and lightning, illuminating for a second the thick black clouds hanging a few feet above our unconscious bodies. The wet, violent weather outside wakes me, along with Jacques's heavy snoring. Despite the fact that his lying beside me had once been the cure for my insomnia and panic attacks, I can hardly sleep tonight with these storms in my head, knowing it's our last night together.

Before bed I tried making love with him one last time, seducing him as best I could but in the end failing. "Making love to you is no longer possible," he said. "My feelings are too mixed with pain." I partly understand, but the lustful rest of me, most of me, doesn't. Only in the superficial sense could I turn him on: he went to the bathroom to jerk off.

His long legs rest heavily on Max's back. Pinned to the bed, the dog confronts me with pleading eyes. I mouth "sorry" and look away. To this day, after a year of unknowingly torturing Max, Jacques still believes the dog enjoys being trapped under his legs, used as an overnight ottoman. It's much too late to state the factual opposite, so I allow Max to suffer one more night.

Unwillingly I glare at the beautiful morning before Jacques joins it. The first color I see is blue in the sky through the white metal blinds, the happiest of blues, outgoing-iMessage blue—*Blue is the Warmest Color* is his favorite film. The dog managed to escape the legs sometime in the night. Lying along my back, he kicks my ass ever so gently, a change in my breathing pattern giving me away again. I butt the dog's head. "Go to sleep. Ten more minutes," I whisper sweetly, hoping I don't wake my soon-to-be ex.

I'm lying against him, on him, leg draped over his as he snores gently: a generally sound sleeper, no mumbling mind, no real work today or any day. Maybe he has a business breakfast or has to deal with the stress of finding another C-celeb in the city to help him tape for some "crucial" audition he needs to send to L.A. by the west coast afternoon or wonders if he can fit in an acai bowl and green juice at Juice Press before a meeting with his personal trainer. And whenever he is on the clock, it's just hair and makeup and make-believe, star pussy and cock, cigs and coke and signing autographs for waiters and restaurant patrons at nightly wrap dinners. But I breathe him in, sweat and Tom Ford, and the ripe hot air he exhales through his nose. I'm really going to miss this. I'm going to miss him. Turning his head to face me, he breathes in deeply, mumbles something in French.

"What? Why are you speaking in French."

"Why are you speaking in English?" he asks, annoyed.

"Jacques, I think you're dreaming." He opens one eye, then the other.

"Oh, it's you," he says, as if he were expecting to wake up and find someone else. He kisses me on the cheek. I beat the thought of him with another lover out of my mind. On his back he stretches his arms and legs the way my dog does when waking peacefully—Max had retreated to the bathroom the second Jacques stirred—then wraps all appendages around me like an octopus. His morning hard-on pokes my thigh, turning me on, but he immediately retracts his body from the waist down. Somehow the rejection, this imminent end, is okay today. "So this is it, pretty one," he whispers with bad breath that I greedily inhale, feeling a bit sentimental myself. He kisses my cheeks, my forehead, everywhere but the lips.

"I should get ready for work," I say without looking at him, trying to pull away, but he keeps me locked in.

"Promise me you'll be okay. That you'll take care of yourself. *I need to know this.*" He pleads with moist eyes, as if filled with despair. I'm quite well at this moment with him holding me, so I promise.

He releases me, grabs his phone, his immortal ambitions and the very real chance of super stardom whisking him away from this final moment of our love. I'm realizing it's all he wanted: to be relieved of responsibility, to return to himself. A thick regret seeps into my veins. I try to ignore it, rushing to the shower, feeling thankful I can take a real one. The tiles have dried.

I'M REMEMBERING THE time he had left for Italy, the day after our first fight. I was on a shoot for Scent-Ease, harassing the creatives to stay on track while they agonized over every product shot: horizontal, vertical, the bottle spraying, the bottle not spraying, stills of it on a messy nightstand of twin teenage boys, in a bedroom littered with strategically placed dirty socks and underwear. A text from Jacques: *I'm leaving in an hour! Got cast in the movie after all, but playing the priest... where are you? Can you come say goodbye?* The anxiety python stirred in my stomach as the creatives bitched in my ear about Rosemarie poorly managing the client:

"She's letting him look over our shoulder and nitpick every fucking shot. You have to get him out of here if she won't... Hello? Are you even listening to us?!"

"I have to go," I said. "Family emergency." I put the producer intern in charge, handed her my walkie and shot list, rushed out.

I'd never cycled so fast in my life, was nearly hit by a truck when I ran a red light. By the time I arrived home I was drenched in sweat, my legs trembling. Hobbled up the stairs to my building, barged into my apartment hyperventilating and discovered him all smiles, zipping up his suitcase. Heard a horn outside, and his phone rang. The cab was already there.

"Pretty one..." he said, pulling me to him. "It's only a month."

"A month! Oh god, no. Please don't leave. Please don't leave me!" I broke down in tears, body convulsing violently. Couldn't breathe. He brought me to the bed, laid me over his legs.

"It's okay. Shhh. This is my work, pretty one. I have to go. We'll text every day and Skype when we can, okay? And Max will be with you." He started crying, too. "This is hard on me as well, you know. But we already found each other. We'll see each other again soon."

Felt my phone ringing in my pocket. Work calling, I was sure. My responsibilities were a million tons heavier: returning to the set, waking alone again for at least the next thirty days save for the company of my animal, my demons and the excruciating silence I'd always known.

WHEN ROSEMARIE NODS her head in disapproval—at minimum a half-dozen times a day—her long, dark hair shimmers as if she were in a Pantene commercial. Other observations: a conventionally pretty face, cherry-painted lips that accentuate refrigerator-white skin and complement the raw selvedge denim she's wearing, which suffocate her shapely legs and are paired with knee-high rubber boots, no doubt pulled on this morning because The Weather Channel app gave her an excuse for it by predicting a thirty-two percent chance of rain when she woke up, although it couldn't have been drier all day. Now it's mid-afternoon: the sun's out and not a cloud in the sky. I'm betting her unnecessary footing is eating her insides, given the extreme Type-A she is.

She and I were friends once. It's difficult not to become close when working under such pressure—the countless productions, temperamental clients, trying personalities from other departments—especially Creative—followed by endless drinking and coking up after work—but the line between professional and friendly had begun to blur. When stress came between us at the office, it was difficult to communicate as co-workers. Our companionship came to an abrupt end the night we found ourselves in a private booth at a karaoke bar and she confessed she'd been in love with me for a long time. I didn't feel the same for several reasons—she was married and a co-worker, and I'd never been attracted to women. I'd told her as much as she tore off her top and tried raping my face with her mouth. Bouncers caught her undressing via the security cam below the TV, while the lyrics to "Leather and Lace" by Fleetwood Mac trailed up its screen, and tossed her out on the street kicking and screaming, a mortified me following several feet behind. The next day she was back to her perfect self: no evidence of a hangover or her confession of love the night before except that she was all cold business with me and has been ever since.

At Hustle, in the conference room with the mice-and-earth-worm wallpaper, she's demanding I have our over-allocated resources shoot, retouch and deliver new content for Scent-Ease's paid Instagram efforts by close of business tomorrow—six shots each for the "What's Under My Nose" and "Finish that *Scent*ence" themes—not to mention the website updates due by end of day today. In addition, within the next two hours, for her 4PM call with the client, she's expecting me to provide my vendor recommendations, cost estimates and timelines to build the brand's first mobile app despite the fact that we're still in discovery and I'm not slated to complete all that until next week.

I'm sitting here focusing on my breathing, waiting for her to finish flapping that dolled-up hole in her face. Last week Fung ordered me via text to stop interrupting people and to tell her, in the most diplomatic manner I could muster, to go fuck herself. There's a zero percent chance I'll have enough time to vet all seven vendors and whittle them down to the four we need to power this potential beast of an app concept she's already sold the client without consulting Production or Creative.

I can actually see this anger she's catalyzing in me collecting above us like bees forming into a swarm. Then I think of this morning and Jacques, our final goodbye, how he left Us without taking the sphere ice mold I'd bought him for Christmas, the ball of frozen water that is still in my fridge going stale. It feels the way a one-season series finale leaves me with forever unanswered questions, forcing me to question my illogical commitment to a network show I knew wouldn't be extended because of its low ratings. And the only thing I gained was regret for wasting time.

Thinking back through the last year, I can only remember a handful of moments when we were happy: the Airbnb at Hunter Mountain, until he made Max shit himself out of fear and found it hysterical rather than expressing remorse or comforting the dog; that first night we did coke and fucked at the construction site where the Domino Sugar factory used to be because our liquored, powdered selves couldn't wait the ten-minute walk to my apartment; hungover and crying to *Derek* on Netflix as we compared our dysfunctional family histories to the main character's, especially mine, and he more lamenting mine than his own because he didn't really have one in his mind.

He's always projected this air of sophistication around me, but the truth is he grew up middle-class in the suburbs of Canada. His dad was a car salesman who saved enough to buy a few buildings in Montreal, eventually turning a moderate profit in commercial real estate, chucking away the job and older wife and moving to Marseilles when Jacques was twenty-one. The ex-wife, a former waitress and stay-at-home mother who pushed him into child acting, that so-called classy woman who was much too refined for him to introduce to lowly old me, a woman who never finished college but continues to get by, he once told me, on paltry alimony payments and bad online dating. It's no wonder he insists on being the ultimate expert on fine wine and food, why he's perfected his French accent and learned how to hide the Canadian twang to get better roles in European films. He also speaks Spanish fluently as a result of college classes and an extended backpacking trip throughout South America.

None of this bothers me. I, too, have done my fair share of hiding the less-than-chic facts of my past in order to mix with my professional peers, but never would I impress my manufactured sensibility on the real people in my life. Maybe he wouldn't, either, which is probably why he has left me here alone, with no one but my dog and my thoughts, because he doesn't consider me important enough to be honest. The lovely morning, the tear-and-saliva-streaked goodbye as he cupped my cheek with the hand he punched me with the night before, promising me that wherever he'll be in the world making his next movie, no matter how alone I'll feel at times—like right now—I must remember there's someone out there who thinks I'm amazing and beautiful.

The mice-and-earthworm wallpaper, the mice and their little beady eyes, the worms without a face who are nevertheless watching—I know they can see me, I fucking know it! The Eyeballs from last night, the Official Fucking Eyeballs. They're all still here, glistening and gloating. I'm alone. I'm alone. Eye'm alone! "Fuck!"

"Um, excuse me?" Rosemarie goes from talking at me to actual milliseconds of looking at me.

I missed a step. I'm remembering the morning, the sweet morning: Showered. Cried goodbye. Dressed. Grabbed bike from balcony. No, after he left I walked the dog first… grabbed the bike from the balcony. But I've missed a step: Didn't pop a couple Advil, two lithium, one Zoloft and two Klonopin. Not that skipping one day of doses will push me over the edge. Or has it been a week? Today is definitely Tuesday—I know this because our weekly status call with the brand was this morning. But was yesterday the Monday Jacques and I broke up, or was it the previous?

"Nothing, I… I ha-have to go," I say timidly, demonstrating a personality that is the polar opposite of the headstrong one I usually exude during business hours. The only other time I appeared this weak was the morning after a midweek, late-night coke binge as well as a big bottle of Maker's, with Jacques, knowing I had to lead an 8AM call with London but being tempted anyway with his toxic booty. It happened after he'd returned from some movie premiere at MoMA—one I hadn't been permitted to attend with him; he'd gone with a forty-year-old Canadian actress I'd never heard of. At work the next day, on no sleep, still a bit high and drunk, I chalked up my sweats, shakes and frequent trips to the restroom to check on my pallor and dilated eyes to food poisoning.

Her nose wrinkles, upper lip snarls as if she were just treated to a Dirty Sanchez. "O…kay? Is there someone who's going to cover for you while you're out? I mean, I just downloaded you on everything, and now you're telling me you have to go?"

"Sorry, I'm late," Fung says, barging in.

Rosemarie immediately perks up. "Well, hello there, lady! Just in time," she says through a glorious smile, although there's nothing in the eyes. They're empty, soulless, like those of a wildcat. She's beautiful, but she'll claw you to death when you least expect it. "We were just discussing a backup plan for—"

"Fung, I have to head out early. I was going to come find you after this. I'll do what I can from home via email and address the rest first thing tomorrow," I say.

Today Fung's attired differently, her matte black hair let down and blown out, a pale blue baby doll dress hiding her chubby figure, topped with a big black bow around a white-collared neck, nude fishnet stockings and the same black-and-white-checkered tennis shoes from yesterday.

"But your out-of-office schedule is not on the team calendar," Fung says. "Did you forget to add?"

"No," I reply, "but—"

"I mean… this is just *not* going to work, Fung," says Rosemarie.

"God, can you please shut the fuck up for *one* minute!" I growl. My panicked state is turning into aggression like a dying dog as someone nears it. Rosemarie scoffs with an upturned nose: the most popular girl in school affronted by the poor alterna-kid.

Fung orders me out of the conference room. As Rosemarie closes the door behind us, she and I make brief eye contact, a shit-eating grin painted on her face, a murderous look on mine.

"What the hell is going on with you?" Fung implores. "You can't speak to your coworkers like that."

"You're right," I concede, worried about my job. If I lose one more thing, I don't know what I'll do.

"It can't happen again. Next time we'll go to HR." My one hard rule at work is no emotion, especially the weak ones, and I'm breaking it. Eyes watering, I think of that song "Water Me" by FKA Twigs, the lyrics racing through my mind as if it were playing on a cassette tape being fast-forwarded. Deep breath. Speak.

"I've got personal stuff going on, should've taken the day off."

She's already in another world on her phone, tapping away, the irritating keyboard sound unmuted.

I'D LIKE TO say I was okay during the times Jacques had been away shooting, that I accustomed myself to living solo as I'd been doing before we met, and since Pedro had died. Instead I spiraled out of control: found myself at the apartments of homely strangers at ten in the morning on a Tuesday or Wednesday, snorting rails off two or three cocks at once, calling out of work at the last minute, claiming a grape-poisoned dog or an injured shoulder in a CrossFit class the night before, whatever excuse popped into my head first.

The paranoia I cultured those high mornings carried into the rest of the sober workweek. When Jacques didn't respond to a text within a half-hour, I imagined all sorts of scenarios in which he was being unfaithful: falling in love with some celebrity princess he'd met on set, having completely lost interest in me now that I was out of sight. I'd send ten more pleading texts before he'd call back to clarify he'd been shooting or in hair and makeup when I'd messaged him. I'd try to explain that it was my mental health issues that made me react the way I had. He'd comfort me, want to understand, but he also said that maybe someone with his career wasn't good for someone like me. I'd convince him otherwise, that I just needed time to adjust when deep down I knew I'd never get used to him being gone. We must've had the same conversation over text and phone a dozen times while he was away, his believing, caring tone gradually degrading to impatience. I knew I was losing him, but I couldn't escape my state of desperation, the neediness boring into my chest like a jackhammer until we could be together again.

THE INSTRUCTOR IS reciting standard Vinyasa techniques as if she were reading them from a textbook. A donation-based organization, Yoga to the People seems to employ only those just taking on the yoga teaching profession. Not that I'm complaining. I rarely carry cash, so I often have nothing to fork over at the end of these basically free classes, including this one. I'm always sneaking past the instructor who stands by the exit with an empty tissue box. Tenderly she speaks:

"Wherever you are in your mind, let it all go, any worry in your personal lives, all the stress of living in this bustling city. As you come into Child's Pose, I want you to exhale, and for the next sixty minutes or so focus only on your breathing, becoming one with your body. Breathe in…

"…and exhale *Om.*"

"*Ommm,*" responds the class in unison, a few of them dragging out the "mmm."

I want to say, "Shut the fuck the up, you've exhaled already, Jesus!" but I imprison my tongue behind clenched teeth, deciding not to express the black rage surging through me, perhaps explaining yoga's ineffectiveness in soothing my nerves.

The instructor continues directing our bodies with her words and various cuckoo sounds, the room—except for me—

following seamlessly along. I have yet to memorize the movements associated with the names of these poses. At every transition I'm mimicking others and only getting halfway through before they're on to the next move. The people breathe out, poisoning the studio. Condensation is clouding the closed windows like crystal meth in a beaker, quarantining from the real world this clandestine lab where we're expelling our toxins, any worry in our personal lives, all the stress of living in this bustling city.

But tonight my psychic pimple is buried deep beneath my mind's skin, incapable of draining. The harder I work on my body and the mental release the instructor is forcing me to fight for, the further the demonic infection burrows into my brain, the unnatural loss of my parents and Pedro and Jacques power-drilling deeper, my angst with the ad agency and failed connections hammering in. My neighbor is lined up too closely with my mat. When he changes to Warrior II his hand touches mine. I want to mutilate him beyond recognition.

After what feels like centuries, the instructor asks us to lie on our backs for Corpse Pose. Everyone obeys in silence, directing their lid-covered eyeballs at the ceiling. I don't. I'm playing dead wide-eyed in clothes saturated to the skin with what my body is secreting—just dirty water, no pain or stress—as if Jacques had violently drowned me in a pool and then dumped my body here while the rest of the class died peacefully in their sleep. The instructor reads a quote from somewhere. I've forgotten to pay attention. It could've been a message for me, a sign, but I'll never hear know it now. She bangs her tiny gong, rolling the tip of a mallet around a metal disc to really drag out its sound, reminding me of those exaggerated *Om*'s from earlier. I want to cry but can't.

Pass-slash-Go paying the instructor at the door like a game piece in *Monopoly*. Don't look at her or say thanks. Check phone. Nothing from Jacques. Remove T-shirt and shorts. Clothe sticky, smelly body in a dry black T-shirt, black sweatshirt, black ankle socks, black jeans, black windbreaker, black boots.

HE'D RETURNED FROM the shoot two days before his thirtieth birthday. I greeted him with an immediate fuck and a fresh bottle of Oud Wood, his favorite scent from Chanel, with a card attached that said, *I'm sorry for driving you nuts in Italy, will make up for it in New York*—had planned on shipping it to him, but he was back early. His birthday fell on the upcoming Fourth of July weekend. He mentioned more than once how he'd always spent it with close friends from home and wanted to this year as well—not to mention he'd already missed Canada Day.

"What about me? You met me. I'm in your life now... I mean you just left."

"Please don't make me feel guilty about this. And I'm here now. Besides, I haven't totally decided."

"Or why can't I come with you?"

"Do you really think I would want that after how you behaved when I was shooting these past few weeks?"

Later in the night, drunk and high, he admitted he'd considered not returning at all and that if I acted the way I had ever again he'd leave me for good.

MUST BIKE HOME to walk Max but find myself in the front row of a theater at Nitehawk Cinemas. There are a total of four short rows in the room and a small screen the size of a giant TV playing *Wild Tales*, an Argentinian film by Damián Szifrón: vignettes of revenge doled out violently, ranging from politically charged motives to passionate ones, most of which I can relate to, particularly in the last story. A jilted bride discovers on her wedding day that her newly acquired life partner kept a mistress during their engagement, and the woman is there at the reception! The bride subsequently beats the mistress and husband to a pulp and then fucks a random member of the banquet staff on the roof. But in the end they reconcile on the dance floor: hardcore fucking for family and friends to witness.

The comfort of the loving goodbye from Jacques, the high of affection, has completely faded. His absence, this comedown, is unbearably palpable. I'm wondering what he's doing right now, whether he's feeling even somewhat comparable. He didn't text from Montreal to let me know he landed safely like he did when we were still in a relationship, that he misses me after all and has a second audition for one of the countless big-budget-movie roles I helped him tape his first audition for and I'm the first person he wants to share the exciting news with. The ritual and responsibility of keeping me in the loop of his vain life has been permanently broken and dissolved. Panic has set back in, so I'm taking out my iPhone, texting him manically to see if he's okay. I need to know he's still there in some way.

Leaving the phone's sound on while cycling home, I take deep breaths till I hear a jingle notifying me I've received a text. I swerve abruptly to the right, nearly colliding with a baby carriage that's materialized from the front of a parked car. The irresponsible Hasidic woman pushing it gives me a nasty look as I say sorry, go around her and come to a complete stop. Frantically checking for his message, I'm assaulted by the sight of a text from my brother Mickey instead. He, his wife and their newborn baby want to come visit me on or before Easter. Though we aren't religious, and this is the first time he's messaged me in months. I don't fucking get why he's suddenly reaching out. It's as if the universe compelled him to do so at this inopportune moment just to torture me, when I'm desperately waiting for Jacques's text. I punch the screen to delete the message. An intimate moment with family, which I equate with their physical presence rather than a passive text of *hello/how are you* now and then, is the last thing I need right now.

FIREWORKS HAD EXPLODED from the roof of my building where neighbors were hosting a party. Held my dog tightly as he violently shook with fear at the loud sounds. We lay in the dark of my apartment like slugs under a rock, the lights in the sky brightening the room for a second or two every few minutes, much to my irritation. Texted Jacques at exactly midnight—as his birthday was the next day, on the fifth. *I'm so glad we met and are together, can't wait to see you again XXX!* Made it sound as if I were doing just fine on my own, when all I'd done for hours on end was wait in agony to hear from him. He responded after 4AM with a mere smiley face emoji, called the next night around seven congested from coke, having partaken in I'll- never-know-what-or-who-else.

MAX'S EXCITEMENT AT my arriving home is just as bad as receiving the unwanted text from Mickey. My dog is whimpering with joy, jumping around me, trying to climb my legs, leaving a trail of white fur down my black jeans. His seasonal process of blowing the white undercoat of his otherwise reddish fur has begun, and it's not even hot yet.

Quick dog walk: holding his leash out the front door of the building so he can piss and shit at arm's length of me, and not cleaning it up. Left the phone charging in the apartment like a pot of water to boil on the burner, hoping a few minutes away from it will bring forth the antidote for my aching heart. Returning upstairs is disappointing: still no word from Jacques. Max is pushing around his empty stainless steel bowls. The sound of them scraping the worn parquet floor communicates a nightmare to my ears: an aural ice pick raping.

"Fucking quit it!" I scream in a monstrous voice.

With a collapsed tail between his legs he darts under the bed like a spooked mouse, his whimpering more like squeaking. A version of remorse comes over me. I get on my hands and knees beside the bed and drag him out while he trembles like a Parkinson's patient. Holding him tightly in my arms, I go through the motions of comforting a pet: massaging the tense muscles around his neck, kissing the top of his head, apologizing profusely for losing my temper. It's as if I'm beside myself, watching myself doing it, because none of it feels sincere. It's more of an obligation. To stay cool with karma, I must be kind to this creature, or I'll never hear from Jacques again.

Release Max, satisfied with my penance. From my black backpack retrieve my work laptop, sweaty yoga T-shirt sticking to it. Peel it off and open the computer while sitting cross-legged on the floor, hoping that answering some work emails will get my mind off things for a bit. Outlook has been infected by seventy-six unread messages, the most recent ones from Rosemarie with aggressive subject lines like *Timelines!* and *DUE NOW* and *Are you joining this call???* It's after six, and I've done nothing. A few of the earlier emails are from the creatives asking for help, begging me to act as a buffer between them and Account, but I can't do it now. As I'm going through them another comes in from Fung that just says *Where are you?* followed by a text message with the same note. If I weren't waiting to hear from Jacques I'd throw both the phone and computer out the window.

Max is pushing around his bowls again because I never got around to feeding him. The more he nags the more frustrated I become and the less motivated I am to satiate his hunger. Moving reluctantly to the kitchen area, I open the cabinets, discovering I'm out of dog food anyway. Grab shredded cheese and moldy pasta from the fridge, plop it directly on the floor. There are pills in the bathroom, but medicating my nerves would be false relief. Need Jacques, the real stuff.

Close the Mac, pick up the phone, flop on the bed face first. Use pillow for a sleep mask because it's not dark yet, and it also muffles the dog's messy chewing, which sounds like choking—he must really be shoving it down. Place the phone by my head and try passing this excruciating wait with a snooze—a nap quickly trampled to death by a rolling stampede of The Eyeballs. Dirt in the air from the road is clouding their vision—but they never blink or stop staring at me.

I stand statued at an intersection, each direction leading nowhere, waiting to be toppled. To them I'm just a bowling pin wrapped in skin and filled with blood and guts. They barrel toward me, their friction with the ground making no sound other than a squish when they graze against each other. This moist ocular army slimes me, getting parts of me stuck between lids and eyeballs, the road burning off my skin as the rolling parade drags me to my death, filling me with equal doses of terror and fury. I want nothing more than to grow fifty feet tall and stomp them out, splatter their parts all over the fucking street. They should've left me alone, refrained from eyeballing, stopped intimidating and violating me, sneaking inside my head like mice with flexible vertebrae that nibble at my nerves and—the ping of a text—an electroshock to my head.

My eyes pop open like a vampire's at the stroke of sundown. I snatch my phone, read the push notification: Jacques! Use my thumbprint for instant security clearance. Move the same thumb to the Messages icon and tap, scroll… scroll… there he is:

Are you there? I'm here in Canada. I'm ok

I stare at the text for a good five minutes, relieved he's finally here but horribly disappointed by the message and unsure how or if I should respond. I'm ignoring Fung and Rosemarie's messages piling onto his.

Jacques: *Hellooo? I wasn't looking at my phone, and then it ran out of battery. And I didn't want to have the same conversation again.*

Me: *By my asking if you landed safely?*

Jacques: *The one we're having now / Reporting to you*

Me: *You're not. I just wanted to know if you made it to Canada.*

Jacques: *I told you ten times I was going!! / You're just investigating me / Which I don't appreciate*

Me: *I was so worried about you all day.*

Jacques: *My phone was dead / Whatever im ok… / I thought we had said goodbye as lovers*

Wherever he is, he feels so close now. It's as if he's in bed next to me, speaking those acid words into my ear, our heads under a shared pillow. He's on his back, and his eyes are covered by it. I'm on my side, staring up at him as the tiny daggers with their tips piercing The Eyeballs fly at me, aimed like pre-programmed torpedoes.

Jacques: *Are you ok?*

Me: *Yeah, I'm fine.*

Jacques: *…*

Me: *What?*

Jacques: *I wanted to reach out sooner but thought maybe I should wait.*

Me: *It's fine.*

Jacques: ...*Had an allergic reaction to some Chinese food at lunch (expensive restaurant though). Took Benadryl so almost better.*

Me: *Ugh that sucks.*

Jacques: *How was work?*

Me: *I left early and went to a film, Wild Tales.*

Jacques: *Oh I've been wanting to see that.*

Me: *Yeah it's great. It's all different revenge vignettes. I feel like they could make it into a cool tv series one day*

Jacques: *I just checked. It's playing at ten-thirty. I have plans with an old friend later so will go do that.*

Me: *Okay*

Jacques: *Pretty one... don't be sad. / I'll text you soon ok?*

Me: *Okay*

Jacques: *Xxxx*

The cure for my worry is just a deadlier disease. His electronic kisses symbolize the Death of Us. I do not believe he means love. Jealousy at the thought of him sharing my movie with someone else instigates a frantic Google search to find the showtimes in Montreal. I vaguely remember reading when I watched the trailer at the office earlier that it's only playing in New York and LA. Cinéma du Parc, Cinéma Banque Scotia Montréal, Cinéma Guzzo: no *Wild Tales*. Dollar Cinema shows only second-run films, I read, so that's a definite no. But there *is* a ten-thirty screening at Nitehawk where I saw the film this evening, and a ten-fifteen at Landmark Sunshine on the Lower East Side. The motherfucker is still here sneaking around *my* city, escorting someone else to *my* movie!

My hands are trembling, evil butterflies attacking my guts. I've gone temporarily blind like when eyes adjust to sudden darkness. Releasing a long, throaty moan of pain, which probably sounds like a very vocal orgasm if my neighbors are listening, I slowly accept this hateful new world: when I look back at Max he's sprawled out on the floor in a dark pool of water beside the stainless-steel bowls, his tongue hanging from his mouth like a playful emoji. Stuck on the bed, like a morbidly obese person confined to a deeply dented couch, I'm incapable of rushing over to check on my best friend, unsure if he's had a bad reaction to the food and choked on it or if my tantrum broke his heart or if he's just taking a nap. "Max!" I call, receiving no response. Other than some fur shifting from a strong, cold wind blowing in through the balcony door, he's not moving.

The sun disappears completely. "Fast Car" is playing from one of the apartments behind mine—I can't tell which. Tracy Chapman's pained voice is volleying against the buildings. I'm feeling envious of whoever's listening to that classic song, someone likely in the final stage of a cancelled relationship: accepting he's not the one, smart enough to forgo the steps that would've cemented a casual lover into something more permanent and then ended in a regret-filled future. I'm in my dark cubby with a potentially dead dog, rejected and lied to by an ex-boyfriend whom I needed to spend the rest of my life with. But in this moment Jacques's crimes are providing comfort because if I did kill Max it's his fault. He must pay.

Ripping myself from the superglue of defeat restricting me to the bed, leaving behind the last shred of my emotional defenses, I plant my feet on the hardwood, make my way to the kitchen area, asking after Max again but not looking down, not ready to know the truth and let guilt pollute my rage. I hear his empty bowls scraping the floor. He could be doing it with one outstretched paw, acknowledging his name but too sleepy to rise; or it's just the shrieking wind assaulting the long white fabric panels covering the door, adding to the chill of the worst day of my life.

I'm eye level with the door to the freezer, a mortuary housing the remains of my relationship with Jacques: the sphere-shaped ice mold I bought him for Christmas. Phone on my bed's ringing. I can make out Fung's name on the screen from here. I'm shivering, and sweat's materializing on my forehead; my muscles are aching. This isn't influenza. It's his influence on my physical health, the stress of his betrayal attacking me like a virus. I hate him. I hate Fung, and I hate myself for what I did to my dog, and now Rosemarie's calling, elevating my tension to a level I've never experienced before. A dose of such distress can surely trigger a stroke if endured by someone in worse shape who is older or overweight. All that biking and those gym classes must be keeping me alive, to correct Jacques's infraction, carry out a final confrontation with him.

Settling on Nitehawk Cinemas—there's the off-chance he'll be taking his whore to Sunshine but it's less likely because he's probably staying in Bushwick with that fat cokehead friend of his from Quebec who barely speaks English—I begin hatching my plan. It's come to me with immediacy like The Eyeballs during sleep. Despite being conscious, I sense their presence, their disgusting attention in the blackness surrounding me, the unnerving squishy sound egging me on: "Openthefreezer/openthefreezer/openthefreezer," they hysterically chant in their slimy alien language.

With an unsteady hand clasping the handle of the icebox, I consider taking my pills. They're in the black backpack a few feet away, packed with the rank gym shorts still damp with sweat from a week-ago workout, a depleted stick of deodorant and a couple balled-up plastic grocery bags to pick up the potentially late Max's shit. "There has to be another way," I say. First-aid my dog. Block Jacques's number. Save the job. Pop the pills. But then what? A little life packed with work all day, Hulu all night, frequent Tinder fucks, after-work drinks and blow with friends once or twice a week, followed by weekends further under the influence, the days and years running away from me until I eventually crash into a wall, ride my bike into traffic or hang myself from the shower head? I know it's possible to live happily, share yourself with someone else—millions have been doing it for ages, but will I after Pedro and Jacques, the demons and all the others? My parents should've taught me better—of course I could've used their volatile relationship and eventual murder-suicide as a warning sign instead of a roadblock all these years. But I didn't, and now my last chance has probably come and gone, and all that's left is the lingering taste of love, the opposite of this emptiness. A beautiful, sensitive man will never love me again.

Certainly Jacques did once. Back in the Bubble. Before I burst it. How could I fault him for giving up on Us, reverting focus to the superficialities of his celebrated life? I turned him, Us, me into silly things. I'm no better than one of his many intrusive fans spotting him on the street. What a hypocrite I've become: a violently infatuated star fucker. A stranger.

And now there's no way to make it right again, not when he'll be living large in his Downtown L.A. loft, my black heart in a front pocket of his jeans while another person has a hand in them, is pulling out his fat, uncut cock, sucking what once was only mine. Love isn't about ownership. Love is a communion, just like he said, a concept I've never been able to truly grasp because I've been too desperate, lonely, in the Void. Hateful as I am at this moment, wanting nothing more than to destroy him for leaving me.

Open the freezer. Take sphere-shaped ice mold into hands. Allow the coldness to hurt them. Become numb. The ball of ice—Heart of Us—is making my hands ache now. The Eyeballs keeping me company gather so closely, their little globular bodies like oversized caviar rubbing against my arms, hands. Their natural juices are acting as a protective lubricant for the pain. Blood rushing from my extremities, coupled with the phone ringing—another call from the office, I'm sure—I come to my senses, realizing I need to return the mold to its brown rubber cover, place it back on the shelf in the freezer and close the door, at least for now.

First I need to pick a transport. The cooler Jacques and I used the only time we went to the beach together comes to mind: the long subway ride to Coney Island in the thick of New York summer when the air conditioner in the car we chose was broken. We were too hungover to move to an adjacent one. While swimming in the graphite-colored water Jacques thought he shook hands with a jellyfish, but it was a condom. Whiplash on the Cyclone. Eating soggy sandwiches from the mini cooler. And later, doing bumps behind each other in the subway station so passersby wouldn't catch us, repeatedly reading a Heineken ad on the other side of the tracks, laughing hysterically: *LONG HOT SUMMER. SMALL COLD CAN. THE NEW 8.5oz SLIM CAN. LONG HOT SUMMER. SMALL COLD CAN. THE NEW 8.5oz SLIM CAN. LONG HOT SUMMER. SMALL COLD CAN. THE NEW 8.5oz SLIM CAN.*

Presently I propose packing the same cooler with ice to transport the Heart of Us, preserving its hardened form till ten after midnight when *Wild Tales* is scheduled to end. He'll be exiting the theater with his hatted head bent toward his chest to avoid any fans who might recognize him—the narcissist. There I'll be, clutching his sphere-shaped ice mold like a baseball, ready to catch him in his nasty lie. Will hurl our love away from me forever, shattering it into icy pieces on the sidewalk before his expensively booted feet, slow time in my mind, relish-slash-suffer every nanosecond of his inarguably beautiful face contorting into the ugly mug of Humiliation. Will carve a permanent feeling of guilt for betraying Us into his mind—or that's the goal. If other moviegoers leaving the same way stop to gawk—likely his accompanying slut and a few nosy fans, if any, given the hour on a Monday night and the tiny size of the screening room—I'll go for their prying eyes like the maniac he made of me because I don't give a fuck anymore. All this right in front of his pale blue peepers, where my amplified persona will live for the rest of his life.

Phone rings again. This time I answer it.

"Yes, Rosemarie. I'm heading back to the office now. I wasn't feeling well, but I'm just going to come in."

"Okay. But you really need to hurry. The creatives' work is on your computer. Umi and Kat are on vacation together, as you well know, and you're the only one with the footage from the L.A. shoot. They're at their hotel in London waiting for you to send it to them, and it's already late-night there."

"Okay."

"The client isn't happy, and neither is Fung."

"Okay! I'll be in!" I scream into the phone. Ending the call, I snatch my keys and wallet from the top of the refrigerator and head for the door, stopping an inch from it as thoughts of my dog reemerge. "Max?" I ask quietly.

Nothing.

Open the door. Rush down the narrow hallway. Avoid college student sauntering by with joint in hand, bombing the communal space with pot smoke. Excluding me, everyone in my building is a spoiled college kid attending Pratt Institute two blocks over. Whenever I say hi they don't look up. The only times they acknowledge my existence are when I have Max with me. They say "Shiba" through giggles, briefly checking him out but never making eye contact with me. I'm not there in their eyes.

During my second lonely week living here, as I lay devastated in bed following Jacques cancelling our holiday in Puerto Rico three hours before our flight because he'd been offered a last-minute gig in some big-budget fag film—the producers had decided to replace some strung-out London heartthrob—I dreamed of dying suddenly, this heart having gone on permanent strike without cause, my human shell decaying in the presence of a growingly hungry dog, my rude neighbors dismissing the rotten smell coming from my apartment. At least the dog would've had sustenance till the stench of me became too potent to ignore and the super had to investigate and called the po-po.

I suppose if it had happened I'd be better off than now, confined to my current situation, greeting with a trembling voice the Dominican owner of the sparsely stocked deli on the corner of my block, asking him if he has bags of ice for sale.

"In the back," he says with food in his mouth. "How are you, my friend?" I avoid looking at him as he sucks the last bit of fried chicken from its bone.

"Okay," I manage to get out. Must act calm. Don't attract too much attention. He may sense my sinister intentions.

"*Dónde está tu perro?*" he asks chipper-voiced—I told him once while on a manic coke-high I spoke a little Spanish. The fluorescent lights he recently had installed during a rudimentary renovation of the store are bearing down on me as if I were being interrogated by a detective. Can he see my heart pounding beneath my black T-shirt?

"Ha, no Max today. He, uh, we went on a long walk earlier. He's passed out at home." I lug a bag of ice from the back cooler to the high counter behind which he sits, presiding over me like a judge.

"Having a party tonight?"

"Uh, heh, yeah. Just a small gathering."

"Pack of Parliament longs too?"

"Sure, if you have 'em."

"Yes, of course, my friend. I always order for you."

Take the change in his outstretched hand. Take it. Take it!

"You okay, buddy? Starting the party early, I see." As he laughs open-mouthed, the two spaces where a couple of molars once lived are black holes sucking me into a hypnotic hell. His muffled voice is barely audible through these ears operating at fifty percent. I'm not okay. Nothing is okay. It never will be again.

A smile. Make a smile. Bring it to life, a paraplegic escaping his wheelchair, miraculously saved by the Holy Preacher of Fear of Being Committed Before Attempting Suicide.

"Ha ha. Ya got me."

"Okay, take it easy, my friend. The night is very young!"

I carry the bag of ice infant-style back to my apartment, its low body temperature numbing this chest Jacques often bruised during arguments and rough sex. My body was spotted with purple bruises for our entire relationship. The biting, the punches, sometimes playful, sometimes not, he was marking me, Us, for Death.

The apartment, blackened by night, greets me with a similar violence, a visual reminder of the nightmare of my solitude. Never in my life have I felt so alone as I do now.

HIS APARTMENT HAD been available for him to move into by the time he'd gotten back from Canada two weeks after his birthday. He'd blamed his delayed return to me on a voiceover recording he had to do for the outdoor scenes in the Italian movie. Sound during the shoot had been shoddy due to a windstorm. He could've just been avoiding New York and me till he was finally able to move into his own apartment.

We started up again semi-normal: fucked and were together every day, but it was rough sex and he was much less affectionate than he'd been in the beginning of our relationship. I pushed the thought of losing him aside, focused instead on helping him get situated in his new space.

There was a lot to do: renting cars, picking up furniture, shopping for home accessories and necessities, Ubers to The Home Depot, painting accent walls. The construction workers had taken so many dumps in the toilet before the plumbing had been turned back on it took me nearly four hours to scrub out the multiple layers of caked-on shit. The more I inserted myself into the move the more distant he grew.

"It's just too much, everything you're doing for me. We're not moving in together, and you're acting like it. I don't want to owe you anything…"

"You don't and you won't," I promised. "I just want to be there for you. You don't know many people in the city, and I want to do this."

He continued accepting my help, albeit begrudgingly, likely feeling he had no choice because he had no one else in the city.

Soon he was offered a role as a guest star in the first episode of a new Canadian TV series of which his female ex was the lead, and had to leave again for three weeks. He was playing a soldier who dies during a fictitious World War III, leaving his wife to raise their children in a war-ravaged country. The parallel romance in the show to the very real five-year history between the actress and him was enough to make me lose my mind—she'd been his girlfriend up until about six months before he and I had met. I tried comforting myself with the fact that he'd left me the keys to his place, inviting me to stay there while he was away. I'd offered to wait for the delivery of furniture he'd bought online. Had slept on the hardwood floor for four days till the bed arrived. Took off one week of work for the gas company scheduled to come Monday, cable Tuesday, and a variety of furniture the remaining days. Spent most of my time staring at the walls, lying face-down on dirty laundry because it smelled of him, staring at my phone, waiting for his daily call or text to report everything I had done for him while he was off shooting a romantic tragedy with his ex-girlfriend. The last four days he was away I only heard from him once.

He seemed heartbroken once he was back in my arms, as if he'd spent those two weeks at the funeral of his soulmate and I was the consolation prize. He wouldn't say a word about the trip, no matter how many times I asked.

I'VE BEEN FIGHTING to keep my balance. The relatively heavy mini cooler is hanging on the left handlebar of my bike, was bouncing all over the place as I rode across the Williamsburg Bridge and potholed Delancey. A chorizo quesadilla calls my name when I pass Taqueria, riding up Orchard. I realize starving myself all day is making me feel worse—not to mention being off my meds—but I can't stop now.

Like any good producer I've mapped out my project timeline: outlined every phase, defined the prerequisites for each step leading up to that immovable deadline. Checked my phone at the light at the end of the bridge, noted three hours and forty-two minutes before having to arrive at Nitehawk back in Brooklyn. Too many minutes to kill. Must pass these seconds busy-brained at the office, away from the confines of my apartment-turned-mausoleum. Between now and then I'm one of those people who work at a hospital transporting donated organs to bodies in need, but I'm not good at my job: the Heart of Us will be dead on arrival. In the Igloo it sits in a bed of ice, remaining intact for now.

At Hustle the overhead lighting is dim in some places, completely off in others, the eighth floor seeming empty of people. In the lobby the security guard working the late shift didn't look up as I entered. He was busy on his mobile, whispering heatedly to someone, mostly likely his kid: "Do your goddamn homework. I don't care about your shows... what you say to me?" And the turnstiles have been broken for a week now, so I didn't have to swipe my building ID to get inside. If some unauthorized person, a thief or a rapist, entered unseen just as I have, the guard would surely be fired without the possibility of unemployment benefits.

Before sitting down at a table in the open-seating-plan office—long tables carved out of giant tree trunks so we look like a flock of osprey balancing on branches; some of the directors have seat cushions crocheted to look like birds' nests—I carry the cooler to the kitchen, ripping open the left side of the refrigerator's double doors, accidentally slamming the door against the wall, but the freezer isn't on the left as I thought. Startling sounds of disrupted plastic bottles and glass jars, unlatched nylon lunch boxes and crinkled paper bags on the shelves on the inside of the door come together in earthquake fashion. Looking down I find the oversized drawer to the freezer. Pull it open. Luckily there's plenty of room, nothing in it except for a half-eaten ice cream birthday cake. Lay cooler inside. Preserve the Heart of Us for a few more hours. Close freezer. Shut refrigerator door—suddenly, Rosemarie! Hiding behind it, thriller-movie style!

"Hi there!"

"Hi."

"Nice of you to stop by. Fung had to fly down to Texas for South by Southwest, so it's just you and me!" she says in an upbeat voice, lacking the facial expression to support it.

"Okay. Well I can only stay about two and a half hours. Need to drop something off to someone at about midnight."

"Nice to see you keeping a commitment," she says between her teeth, walking away straight-backed.

Her snarky words disturb The Eyeballs' nap. Their round bodies roll under closed lids, threatening to open. Keep calm. Get to work.

I go back and forth with Umi and Kat via email. They're the copywriter-creative-director-duo behind Scent-Ease's award-winning advertising campaigns, and real-life lovers. One Japanese, the other Ukrainian, these women speak with such heavy accents it's difficult to decipher what they're saying, so it's always easier communicating electronically. Umi is a great writer for the brand. She's a pro at penning the clever puns with which the client loves to blast their digital display and social media channels. And Kat has a natural eye for pseudo-artistic branding, or should I say a knack for taking credit for the best concepts from the many underlings on her team.

This always baffles me: subordinates keeping their traps shut while their bosses steal their thunder. Just once the broadcast producer on the account attempted the same with me, citing herself in materials for a press release as being the sole producer for an integrated campaign. I replied to the entire team and copied HR, demanding she make the correction immediately and redistribute the deck, which she did begrudgingly. Fung backed me up on that one, but warned me to watch my tone when emailing such a large group. The viral tongue-in-cheek campaign went on to win an award at Cannes—and became the butt of a harmless joke on Colbert, boosting sales exponentially—the agency rewarding each of us with a two-thousand-dollar bonus, which I wouldn't have received had that broadcast bitch gotten her way.

Bitter from my rejection of her come-on, Rosemarie is a vulture, preying on the weak. I could easily push her out of the agency if I had the energy, at the very least get her off the account. For now, I only care about completing the bare minimum, enough to get her and Fung off my back for a few hours. My work history clearly speaks for itself, but producing just isn't my passion at the moment: Jacques is my one and only, and he's bringing me down.

Time passes with me typing email after email, saving assets to the server, drafting contracts for projects incremental to the retainer. I actually forget my lost lover and broken dog for a while, till the alarm goes off on my iPhone and The Eyeballs open up for business. I immediately close my Mac midway through writing an email to Fung, which details a false reason for my recent neglect. Sending it tonight would certainly aid in sustaining my employment, but if I work to finish it now I risk my timeliness to the theater.

Turning the corner, I find Rosemarie slumped over a table, the back of her head in an unnatural position under the spotlight of an overturned desk lamp, the rest of her body less visible in the surrounding darkness of the office. A dark, thick liquid is slowly expanding around her unholy head like a halo of evil. Is it coffee spilt after she passed out? I do know she likes it black, and the brew they have in the kitchen is just weak sludge. Maybe the caffeine couldn't stand up to the thirteen-hour shift she put in today.

However, nearing her, I'm thinking I see a couple of The Eyeballs' reflections in the surrounding puddle. It could also be her permanently open eyes reflected in blood. I felt The Eyeballs stirring earlier. It's possible they woke, gotten to Rosemarie behind my back. Fuck. Fuck. Fuck! Instant sweat announces a panic attack: a sudden, physical-slash-mental sensation akin to the times I thought I'd lost my keys or wallet. It's the not knowing that obliterates my sanity, the wondering how I'll get inside the apartment to walk the dog or unlock my bike from a rack outside the office because the only key was on the misplaced keychain, or in this case, uncertain if my coworker has died. Perhaps it was a stress-related aneurysm like the one Fung had. That doesn't explain the blood, though. Someone could've snuck in and attacked her. She wouldn't have seen him approaching with most of the office lights off, as she was toiling into the late after-hours because of me. If I were pulling my weight around here, this never would've happened—and while Rosemarie isn't exactly my favorite person in the world, I didn't want her to die, not in actuality. It's just too much: Pedro, the demons, Jacques, Max and now this!

There's something wet coming through the laces of my black boots, saturating my black socks, warming my feet. Is it blood? But I too drank countless cups of that shitty coffee all night to stay alert for Jacques, so that's possibly all it is. I don't want to touch the wetness, or her, can't confirm it either way, not when I'm on the verge of being late to the theater.

I'm remembering how I entered the building unseen. I could exit through the emergency stairwell, but there must be security cameras in the lobby. I'm hoping they're out of order, same as the turnstiles. I guess I'll find out in a few hours when the admen and women file into the building between nine and ten AM and discover the bitch's body. Police will probably be knocking down my door for a statement after they watch the electronic eye's recorded testimony. Remains of Max will be found, my immortal shame resting beside him in a doggie-bowlful of fatal mistakes.

A light yelp escapes my lips when my mobile goes off in the back pocket of my black jeans. Other than the threat of solitude, there's nothing and no one of whom I should be frightened except my loathsome self. Fung is calling. For some reason I answer it.

"Fung?"

"Uh yeah."

"Hi."

"Why do you always answer the phone like that?"

"What do you mean?"

"Why do you ask me if it's me when you know it's me. My number's in your phone, right?"

"Yeah it is… I… I don't know. How's Austin?"

"I can't chitchat. I'm between a client dinner and after-party-drinks thing with Punchy. Oh, I told them about the scratch-and-sniff stunt idea. They're into it."

"That's… great."

"You better be at the office. Rosemarie has been calling me all day and IM'ing me on the fucking plane. I don't have time to think for myself let alone referee you two."

"No, no… it's okay."

"I know you've been catching up, saw your emails, so that's good."

"Well, I didn't go in. I've been working from home."

"As long as you're getting it done. I haven't been able to reach your Miss Nemesis all night, so make sure you two connect directly."

"Of, of course, yeah…"

"I'll be sloshed after another hour of cocktails. Then I have to speak in front of about two hundred people at eight in the morning—hold on. What? I'm staying at the W…," she's saying to someone on her end of the line, "the W! Not the fucking *Wyndham*! I told him! You think I'd be caught dead—?" Then the phone is silent and the room is instantly darker, Rosemarie's body deader. Look away. Pack black backpack. Grab mini cooler from freezer and go.

Walking back to my computer, I see twenty-two emails have accumulated in a span of eleven minutes, mostly from Umi and Kat, the others a bunch of follow-ups from Rosemarie's minions working remotely. With an obsessive compulsion resembling being unable to stop cleaning the apartment once I've begun, part of me feels compelled to stay till I've answered all of them, completed this never-ending work.

There are two conflicting, unseen forces at play here: one wanting me to labor, the other needing me to confront Jacques; and the latter is winning. At least I'll be completely aware when I commit the potentially third installment of my relationship killings, unlike the deaths of Max and Rosemarie, those twigs with which I unintentionally fed the blazing fire of my heartache—and hatred.

"YOU HAD ME wrapped around your finger," he had said, as we lay on our backs on his firm mattress, staring at the ceiling. Naked, no eye contact, the morning light intruding through the window. We'd been trying to come down from the partying, but the Klonopin we'd taken over an hour before wasn't working fast enough. Our bodies were making the mattress shake like one of those vibrating cheap motel room beds that run on quarters. "It's ruined now. Just earlier tonight, the way you freaked out over the videos."

"You flat out told me you had a fucking crush on her while we were high on coke, how the fuck else was I supposed to react?"

The Polish bar: us reunited after three months of him being away shooting a film with Bree Harringway, great granddaughter of legendary American novelist Bernie Harringway, showing off video after video on his phone of them driving in a car singing together, lying on the floor in his trailer stoned, making funny faces and laughing uncontrollably, sporadic kisses on cheeks. The anxiety python had come alive, and I had struggled to breathe at the bar, causing quite the scene before ducking out and puking on the street. Seeing him after so long had been hard enough on my nerves—exciting, sure—but extremely stressful, and all he'd wanted to do was talk about this new crush with whom I couldn't compete: I wasn't a movie star.

"I've gotten in too deep with you," he said, lighting a cigarette, adding to the smoke hovering over his bed like dark clouds before a storm.

"We can go back to that. Our Bubble, remember?"

"It's too late for that... Look, I'm going to spend more time in L.A. I think I'm going to move back, actually. My agent is setting up a lot of auditions for me, and there's not enough happening in New York... and you were the only thing keeping me here."

"I could come with you, I'd move there. There are plenty of ad agencies out there, I'd get a job in a second. We could start over."

"I thought about that," he said, turning on his side, back to me. "But I don't want to build a home with you. It's like an addiction, you and me. It's not healthy."

Whimpering, I whispered, "Please don't do this. You don't understand. Losing someone is harder on me than other people. I'm not like other people. I don't think I'll recover." Broke into a full-on sob, but he didn't turn to comfort me.

"I'm so sorry, pretty one." Seconds later he was snoring and I was left with the dark cloud, hallucinations of my dead, bloodied parents sharing the bed with us, and Max desperately scratching at the bedroom door.

TONIGHT AT THE theater will be our actual last date, the final goodbye. It wasn't the sweet morning farewell we had yesterday—or two weeks ago—like he thinks. I won't let go that easily. The butterflies in my stomach playing hardball with my heart: loving him, striking out at him, it's all the same to me. We always used to say, "I hate you," followed by kisses and hugs, sometimes a wild fuck. It was less of a euphemism than we made it out to be.

Our communion had been more like a scene from a bad romance flick: third date at Rye on South Second filling our bellies with a six-pack of oysters, wetting our brains with Old Fashioned's, many of which were comped by the generous bartender. She was a "big fan." I didn't know who he was yet, so I thought she was just hitting on him. As far as I knew, his name was Franco, not Jacques, and he was a producer like me, not a C-celeb-slash-actor—he finally told me the truth that night.

Sneaking out back for a few fags and kisses, twinkling in each other's eyes, the band seeming to be playing the most upbeat blues ever heard by anyone. The people surrounding us bared toothy smiles and happy eyes. Laughter was everywhere: a fairy-tale eatery, the joy palpable, the mania of it all so powerful it could've shattered the glasses and windows at any second of those few wondrous hours. Our unity was a sonic boom.

Torrential rains fell as we walked down Roebling, toward my place. He pulled me down a set of stairs leading to a basement apartment—the lights were off inside—with an awning over the front door to protect us from the weather, where he could maul me in peace. His attack on my heart went unnoticed by the pedestrians on the street above us, speaking in singsong voices as they walked past: *Williamsburg, a Love Story: The Musical,* Starring Jacques and Me.

The Heart of Us was born that night! We were in FKA Twigs-Robert Pattinson love, except ours didn't result in a marriage proposal. Who knows, maybe theirs won't progress any further. There've been online rumors of the pair postponing their wedding due to shifty waters, not hectic work schedules as their PR teams would like us to believe. I hope it's just a front for a promised relationship gone rancid, so I can devour the detritus of their hearts via Trending News on Facebook.

The leftovers of Rosemarie's soul remain where I found them, dead or asleep in a pool of something, same as Max. The security guard didn't chase after me once I got past him down a flight of steps in the emergency stairwell. He must've been doing his rounds when he caught me trying to escape unnoticed: "I don't remember you coming in. Did you check in?" he asked authoritatively, as if a gun were strapped to his waist next to the silent two-way radio and set of keys jangling a Western-faceoff-style tune in unison with his marching up the stairs. Without warning I pushed him to the side, not a word, just a hard shove against the wall and then two steps down at a time until I reached the door. A blinking red exit sign winked at me as I left: the electricity of the building, the energy of the universe encouraging me onward in my very own *Journey to the End of the Night*. No one or nothing can stop me now.

Not even the stretched links on my bike chain, desperately hanging onto the circling gears with rusted, worn-out spikes but losing its grip every time I go over a pothole or one of the count-less bumps along the city's uneven, unfriendly streets. At the shop on Third and A earlier this week, the deteriorating, wiry-framed East Villager with a rats-nest beard and concave eyes told me the only way to stop the chain from jumping off its rollercoaster track is to replace the whole setup, which will set me back a few hun-dred dollars that I don't have.

Considering my inflated salary, I find it odd I'm always broke and live in a shit studio on the border of city-funded housing—last week, at the grocery store around the corner from my place, an overweight black woman asked me to buy her a loaf of high-fructose-corn-syrup bread and a package of mystery meat to feed her and her hungry child, but I couldn't oblige because I barely had enough money for the can of tuna and three-for-a-dollar rolls I was purchasing. An evening of hating myself ensued—for con-stantly borrowing money from my brother, who makes half as much as I do, and from gullible friends I'll never pay back, a result of always overspending on chic dinners to keep up with Jacques's HBO-paycheck-funded lifestyle, his Canadian frugality coming through his always making us split the bill fifty/fifty; restocking clothing in my black wardrobe at the first sign of it fading; and the Almond-Joy-sized mound of china white we ingested two or three times a week, almost every week we spent together these last eleven or twelve months.

Here I am on the northwest corner of a car-chaotic Essex and Delancey yanking the disappointing bike chain onto the dully spiked gear, my fingers getting pinched between the two. Digits split open, blood and black grease darkening my hands. Solving the mechanical trouble for the time being and hopefully long enough to get to Nitehawk sans further interruption, I stare at these hands transfixed by the damage. Rather than finding a Starbucks to wash my hands or a pile of napkins from a nearby pizza joint to apply pressure to the fingers and stop the bleeding, I bring the soiled, wounded extremities to my face, smearing the homemade camouflage under each eye and across my forehead. I'm a soldier on a mission, readying myself for battle, hell-bent on ensuring the casualties of tonight will not have been in vain. The city's civilians crossing the busy intersection sneak in what-the-fuck glances at the scene of me. Leering at no one in particular, I mount my untrusty steed, return the fingerprint-filthy, scuffed-up white mini cooler to the left handlebar and ride on.

Brooklyn bound on the Williamsburg Bridge is not as steep of a cycle as it is going into Manhattan, but it's a much longer one: when traveling from the opposite end of the bridge, the ascent is worse but quicker. And I've always been the type who prefers to rip off a Band-Aid rather than extend its painful removal. In my dark time of anticipation, this familiar trip to my home borough feels treacherous and more strenuous than usual. The electric city skyline is stabbing a ceiling of low-hanging clouds while ogre-faced joggers are coming at me head-on. I swerve around them just in time, also dodging the cigarette bullet a hooded teen-wolf has flicked at me. It lands in an overfull Keep-New-York-City-Clean can, causing a nasty explosion behind me—or was it just the high beams of a truck on the other level of the bridge? A banana peel, debris from the bomb going off or possibly a plop of rain, slaps my back. The tires on my bike feel like they're sinking into the hot tar of what was pavement just seconds ago, but I trudge through it.

Nearing the top of the bridge, I spot a female jogger a few feet away, running on the bike side of the bridge, halted in her tracks by a long-haired white kid on a lowrider BMX who's wearing an oversized white Nike sweatshirt. He emerged from the overpass and has come to a tire-screeching stop in front of her. She freezes as another young one with a platinum buzz-cut comes up behind her and rips away the iPhone she has Velcroed to her upper arm. He jumps on the back of the bike, and they coast down the bridge in grim silence, expressionless. The stricken pink-spandex lady chases after them, but not before giving me a thankless look for standing by and watching the crime as if it were an episode of *Law & Order* on my laptop. Pedaling as fast as I can, I pass them all. Other than a car or two driving by, South Fourth Street and then Berry Street are silent.

Gloomy streetlamps and modern fixtures in the windows of the residential buildings I pass illuminate the path to the only person I ever truly loved and hated. The black garage in front of which an old man usually offers to teach chess to passersby during summer is shut and chained, a warning sign with the words Do Not Even Think of Parking Here spray-painted in piss-yellow across the doors. I can understand his ritual behavior: setting up a vintage wooden table daily, arranging the pieces of his royal court, hanging a block-lettered invitation for free chess classes over the no-parking sign, challenging himself to a few games until someone stops and takes him up on his offer, if anyone ever does. I can only imagine how many weeknights and weekend afternoons he sat at that table opposite no one, waiting in vain. Last summer and the ones before, whenever I biked past him, he was always alone, pushing a piece across the board, mumbling to himself, eyes moving longingly up and down the block, then back to the board where his friends live. Inanimate objects will become family if you're not careful.

At the corner of Berry and Metropolitan, I'm cautiously laying the cooler on the sidewalk to lock my bike to a street sign. The ride here took about twenty minutes, so some of the ice inside could've melted. Protecting the Heart of Us is the immediate mission. Gently shaking the cooler, I hear no sloshing of melting ice, just the sound of the ice cubes keeping the sphere-shaped ice mold. I'll just assume everything's kosher: opening the cooler to double-check would release some of the cold, which brings to mind a painful memory of drunken Dad lashing my back with the buckle end of a belt for leaving the freezer door open while I was deciding on a Popsicle flavor.

The façade of Nitehawk Cinemas sports a static LED light show: row upon row of short lines of white dazzle arranged side by side, tally-mark style. Toward the middle and right the rows space out, forming a swirl, turning right and then up, down, right and around again. Getting closer, I see the maze of clustered lines is not what it seemed. Making up each tally mark are five or six bright-eyed Eyeballs in single file. Their attention focused on me, they've stopped blinking permanently. Empty-stomach bile escapes my esophagus. I'm in front of the bar on the ground floor of the theater—albeit empty, but still open, as evidenced by the bartender wiping down a table—so to anyone happening by I just had too much to drink, which isn't as embarrassing as the truth.

Nor had it been outside of Williamsburg Cinemas, after Jacques and I had seen *Godzilla* in 3D: our first movie date. A short woman with chub peeking out of ill-fitting jeans had provided a real-life example of the body shape known as muffin top.

With her thick left arm, she steadied herself against the back of a matte black Smart Car, vomiting violently on its bumper, spilling some of it on her thin, corkscrew hair hanging over her face like a ratty curtain. He and I had been on our way to the Korean barbeque spot next to the theater—neither of us had tried it before—when we noticed her. I was a human for once, suggesting we stop to see if she needed help, if we should call an ambulance. He'd complained he was famished and that she was probably just some homeless drunk anyway. Normally, he wouldn't have succumbed to his true nature, but we'd only managed to sleep two or three hours the night before, the result of a coke binge that hadn't ended until that afternoon.

"Are you okay?" I said. "Do you need us to call someone?"

With Jacques's expression growing increasingly *Zoolander*, he leaned against a nearby tree trunk to take a selfie with her in the background for his thirty-thousand Instagram followers.

"I'm fine. I'm fine," she retched, waving us away without looking up. "It was the 3D. Gives me motion sickness."

Sharing a silent laugh, Jacques and I had continued toward the restaurant.

Mini cooler in hand, I ascend the staircase to the lofted second floor of the theater, which acts as a lobby and has a full bar—they also offer an extensive menu of food made to order and eat while the film is playing. Approaching a pear-shaped girl with long, straight blond hair who's bent over the bar and talking in a high-pitched voice to the lanky, bearded bartender in a red plaid shirt and overalls, I anticipate a wave of calm nearing the shores of my nervous system, as if the interior of the theater were Jacques holding me in his arms as he's about to plant a fat, wet one on me.

"Excuse me."

She's wearing a boxy, faded black T-shirt, mom jeans and white Keds, an attempt at normcore that falls short of perfecting a fashion style better suited for anorexic runway models.

"Hey," she says, turning around.

"Hi, what time's *Wild Tales* ending? A friend's meeting me. I mean, I'm meeting my boyfriend. He's in there now."

"Whoa, you have black stuff all over your face," she chuckles.

"Oh. Yeah. No, I know," I say, manically wiping it off with the sleeve of my black sweatshirt. "I was fixing my bike outside. Guess I got some on me."

"Watch the bar a sec? Need to piss," the bartender asks.

"Don't fall in!" the girl teases. She is tapping loose-wristedly at a touchscreen at the end of the bar. "Uhhh, lets out at 12:10."

"Great, thank you," I say, feeling the anxiety python in my stomach suddenly coiling. Knowing I'm seeing Jacques soon is too overwhelming. The Eyeballs glaze over my vision, blanketing my surroundings in a translucent quilt of tiny eyes, like a Google AI dream.

"You okay?" The girl's voice is muffled. The Eyeballs are spilling out of her mouth like the rainbow puke filter on Snapchat.

"I'm okay," I lie in my mind, but rather than getting the words out, I projectile vomit, some of it getting on her arm. Before mortification ensues, the assumptive thought of her having caught come by many a man passes through my brain. She lets out a long, high-pitched scream. Keeled over, I try apologizing through dry heaves.

"Aw what the fuck!" asks the returning bartender.

In response, the girl expels cottage cheese chunks on my boots.

"I'm sorry. I'm sorry. I, I'm sick," I say. The girl, bent over, gets an arm over the bar and pulls herself upright. "I'm sorry. I'll help you clean up. Can I use the bathroom?"

"Don't help. Just go!" she says.

Running a white rag under a sink behind the bar, the bartender tells me the men's room is downstairs, which I already know because I was here earlier today and countless times before. Mini cooler secured under arm, I hurry from the room, fearful of ADHD Jacques coming out for a fag and a phone call, as he so often does at the movies, and discovering me in my beleaguered state.

The bathroom mirror offers a sallow-faced me with severe dark circles and a red, swollen upper lip from licking and chewing it with my incisors for who knows how long. A cold sore from the irritation is on its way, I'm certain. What happened? Is this just my nerves? I'm wondering. The step I missed today—or maybe for a whole week—flickers in my mind like a dying fluorescent light: a couple Advil, two lithium, one Zoloft and two Klonopin. I must be suffering from physical withdrawal by quitting cold turkey on my meds and Jacques—on top of the mental side effects.

Seeing Jacques in this state is not an option. With a Parkinson's hand, I rummage through my black backpack, eventually finding the prescription bottles. Pop two lithium, one Zoloft, and two Klonopin. Wash them down with saliva. But this dire situation calls for more than the usual dosage: pop two more lithium, two Zoloft, two more Klonopin. Swallow the heavy load with the help of tap water. That's better.

Better than now, sitting on a stoop outside a brownstone adjacent to the theater, where there's a cardboard sign taped to the railing to which I've locked my bike, politely reading: "Merry moviegoers please don't sit here!"

The mini cooler rests on my lap like Max never did. Despite their canine status, Shiba Inus are more cat than dog, which is why I chose that antisocial breed: he was an extension of me. As beautiful as they are, there's not much to their personality, especially Max's. He would never go to dog parks. The one time I took him he climbed over a wire fence to escape, ran onto Driggs Avenue. He was almost killed by a biker gang rumbling by, but I grabbed him by the tail just in time. He is rarely playful and never affectionate. The most I could expect was his hyper behavior the nights I'd gotten home late. But given his genetics, the bond he formed with me was the best he could do, the only one he ever made. He'd paid absolutely no attention to the many rendezvous lovers that had come in and out of the many apartments in which I'd lived during the seven years he'd been alive—Jacques, the only real union for me, was just another passing fling to him.

There's less than five minutes to 12:10AM and my thighs have gone numb from the mini cooler, the shifting of the ice cubes inside it sounding more like melting ones in an Arnold Palmer than the rock-hard state in which they were earlier. Vision hazy, I glance at the convenience store across the street where I'm sure they sell bags of ice. Using their lashes as arms, The Eyeballs are struggling to pull open my lazy lids, but their skinny extremities aren't strong enough. As close as more ice is, it's so far away...

Wetting the bed isn't just for kids: I wake to a drenched crotch and a cop nudging me with a nightstick, his face hidden in the shadow of a police cap. The darkness that surrounds us is unsettling: I quickly realize I'm still on the stoop and that the static light-show of eyes that decorated Nitehawk is off. Oh my god, they're closed.

"You can't sleep here."

The mini cooler is spilled open on my lap, the sphere-shaped ice mold melted away except for its casing. A few straggling cubes of ice haven't liquefied, but the rest have died with the Heart of Us, soaking my black jeans and underwear. By the smell of it, it's obvious I've pissed myself, too.

"What have you taken?"

"He may need an ambulance," says a nearby voice I can't immediately place with a body. Must be his partner.

"I'm sorry, I must've passed out," is what I thought I replied, but it must've come out garbled.

"Can you stand?"

Grabbing the railing, I pull myself up but fall back onto the concrete stoop, my lower back hitting the top stair. Too many pills to feel the pain, I guess, but at least The Eyeballs have evacuated the building in my mind... for now. The memory of my berating that bicyclist the morning of my last day with Jacques streaks through my brain. Someone speaks into a radio requesting an ambulance.

My next conscious moment is at the hospital—no memory of the ride in the ambulance or being placed in a hospital bed and wired to an IV and catheter—where a nurse is asking me for my social security number.

"058... I'm sorry... can you repeat the question?"

"Your social security number."

"0..."

I wake again, my brother Mickey sitting across from me, eyes closed, head resting in his right hand. His usually hairless head, which he shaves himself, now has dark-brown locks growing unevenly. He's wearing a navy-blue Russell Athletic sweatshirt stained with white paint and, in this dark room illuminated only by the fluorescent light in the hallway, what appears to be spatters of black oil, with plain blue jeans so old and faded they look stonewashed. A stench of body odor and cigarette-smoked clothing envelops the unventilated room.

Tara's in the chair opposite my slouching brother, staring out of a filmy window, her stringy blond locks pulled back into a haphazard ponytail. Vomit decorates the top of her thin white blouse, which is yanked up, exposing a nipple on which a newborn's mouth is greedily sucking. Her loose belly hangs over khaki pants stretched over thighs thicker than they used to be. Neither of the two was ever fashionable, but they were a fairly handsome couple before deciding to get hitched and her knocked up. Now I guess it's all about paying rent, affording diapers, daycare. I bet they don't even fuck anymore. The very thought of the nightmarish predicament into which they may have gotten themselves is further weakening my already damaged body and beaten spirit.

The mattress in this bed is too hard and sans pillow, which I spot on the floor near Mickey's work-booted feet. The pillow looks flat and its fabric abrasive, so I'm sure it wouldn't have prevented the stiff pain in my neck and shoulders, anyway.

"You're awake," Tara whispers.

"I'm fine… Why are you guys here?"

"They called us. You have Mickey as your emergency contact in your phone."

I recall Thanksgiving last year, when drunken me was feeling sentimental—"We're the only family we've got, *blah, blah, blah*"—and Mickey and I adding each other to the medical information in the Health app on our iPhones.

"How are you feeling?"

Mickey stirs, opens his eyes despite our low-volume voices. "There you are."

"I'm fine. You really shouldn't have come."

"Um, they found you on the street OD'd and soaked in piss," he says, "and what was with the cooler?"

"Nothing, never mind."

"They think you tried to kill yourself. I saw Jacques calling so I answered your phone. He was flying from Canada to L.A. early. Guess he was cast in a movie last minute or would've come. He was pretty upset about it."

"It doesn't matter. We're done." Hearing he called and isn't in New York like I thought, and is already on to the next phase in his life while I'm stuck wallowing in the dregs of our relationship finally makes me realize we're permanently over.

"It's probably for the best if this is what it's doing to you."

"I didn't try to kill myself. Took too many pills."

"Well, they say you can't leave till the doctor checks you."

Feeling strangely resentful of their presence, I want to ask him why he's suddenly playing the role of caring older brother. Maybe it's the fear of losing the last blood relative he has. We've hardly spoken lately, which I suppose is as much his doing as it is mine.

"I found your keys in your jeans and went and took care of Max," says Tara.

"What?! Max? He's okay?"

"He is now! But he must've been alone forever, poor thing. Such a cutie, my baby nephew. Oh! And some woman named Rosemarie was texting, asking why you left the office earlier. Your boss?" Now that Tara's a mother, her voice is squeakier, more nails-on-a-chalkboard than before. But it's an immense relief to hear that my dog and Rosemarie aren't dead; at the same time, I'm horrified to learn that much of my memories since going off my meds have been hallucinations on an insanity bender.

"She's not my boss," I say.

"Well, I let her know you're in the hospital."

"Did you tell her why?"

"Just that you had an allergic reaction to your meds. She said she'd back you up while you're out."

"Really? Okay, thanks for handling all that."

"Of course. You know we're always here for you."

Her hand resting on mine is enough to make me lose my mind again, but the drugs I'm still on are helping me control myself. Baby Lacy lets out a visceral scream as she struggles to break free from the Minnie Mouse blanket in which she's tightly swaddled. Tara speaks baby gibberish and shoves her tit back into Lacy's mouth. While sucking, Lacy looks at me for the first time in her life, and I don't know how I feel about it. The sight of her innocent eyes aware of my existence while my brother stands over me is heartbreaking. In vain he tries hiding the deep hurt we've shared since we were kids, aggravated by this recurrence of self-destruction. Suddenly Jacques doesn't matter as much anymore, and our love seems a bit trite; the obsession is dissipating like rain clouds in sunlight.

The first time Mickey and I were in the hospital together was the afternoon our parents died. Dad had killed himself at the house with a single shot to the heart, but Mom hung on in the hospital with the bullet in her head. After a failed operation, she was pronounced brain dead and taken off life support. Beside her hospital bed, Mickey clutched my forearm so tightly it felt as if he'd break it. I was covered in blood from having held our unconscious mom in a red pond in our kitchen while eighteen-year-old Mickey had been on a date with his girlfriend.

Their deaths inspired Mickey to become a responsible adult, a good husband and loving father. He found a job in construction and took over the mortgage payments. Two years younger, I internalized the pain, allowing it to calcify around my heart. The lack of familial resources made me independent, too, but also obsessively ambitious about moving to the city and creating a new life. A conscious effort to forget only strengthened my dark memories: the weekday mornings our perpetually hung-over mother berated Mickey and me before school, suffering through our father's ritual of beatings and begging for forgiveness, her muffled screams while he raped her in the bedroom next to ours, years of fear and violence that led up to her decision to divorce him, and his to kill her and himself in response. Those were my lessons in loving.

"I didn't want you to find out this time, Mickey. I didn't do this for attention…"

"I wish you had," he says, eyes filling with tears. He takes my hand in his, clutches it firmly. It feels like my bones are cracking.

OVER THE YEARS I've mastered psychiatric evaluations. I know just what to say to get out of those mandatory seventy-two-hour holidays in the crazy wards of hospitals. Last night's incident wasn't a conscious attempt on my life, but the doctors could've easily misconstrued it as such had I not handled their evaluation the way I did.

Lying on my bed I'm feeling horribly hung over and saddened by my mild pride in my sociopathic skill set. A curled Max is sleeping at my feet, Mickey's on the balcony smoking and Tara's in the bathroom changing Lacy's diaper on the toilet top. Other than my bed, the only surfaces in the apartment are the hardwood floor, kitchen table and counter. I'm assuming she doesn't want to be rude and wipe up shit where I eat, but I wouldn't have minded.

"This cabinet door is crooked," Mickey says coming back in. He grips the handle, pushes it into place. "Aw fuck, it's all greasy."

"Close the balcony door, babe! It's freezing," she shouts from the bathroom.

"Yeah, it's been like that since I moved in. I scrubbed the whole place down. Guess I need to clean more."

My brother's a contractor, so he thinks he's an expert when it comes to home improvements. Tara emerges from the bathroom, lays Lacy next to me.

"Say hi to your baby niece!"

Max appears at the baby's head, sniffs it manically. With big, unblinking green eyes Lacy looks at me again as if she knows something I don't.

"What kind's this?" Mickey asks. From the middle of the stovetop he picks up an empty bottle of Hungarian vodka that Jacques gave me after returning from filming there. That and the broken zebra-patterned iPhone charger plugged into the wall socket behind me are all that I have left of him. The tail end of the numbing meds I took last night have shrunk my anxiety python to the size of a garter snake, so I no longer feel anything for the remains of our dead relationship… for now. I'm just tired. Tired of reliving our history every day as if I were the star of a psycho-suicidal-themed sequel to *Groundhog Day*. If there were a cure for memory I wouldn't be stuck performing this sad scene ad infinitum.

"Put it next to the garbage, please? Forgot to toss it."

"I'll take care of it," Tara says. "Where's your trashcan?"

She begins collecting balls of toilet paper I'd blown my coke-congested nose in, which are strewn on the floor and countertop. From a drinking glass into a plastic grocery bag serving as a trashcan she pours dozens of wet cigarette butts in black sludge, which I imagine rolling around inside my lungs. Now that Jacques's gone I should get around to quitting.

"There's a chute in the stairwell right outside my front door. Just leave the bottle next to it on the floor."

"You got it, babe!"

We're sitting at a corner table at Dino on Dekalb. Tara's breastfeeding Lacy beside me as I try remembering how we got here—I assume Mickey drove; they would never walk the five blocks—or how long it's been since the hospital. I guess we got out of there around noon. Pit-stop at mine, a nap on my bed with the infant stranger eyeing me with enormous green eyeballs while sucking on her mother's tit, seeming to demand I show my approval, the way Max locks a stare in front of my eyes when he's shitting on the street.

The table's so wide, it's as if my brother sitting across from me is eating alone. He's onto a second order of calamari in complete silence. He never socializes while scarfing down a meal but slips into a daze, an island in his mind where no one can get to him. Tara can't stop talking about how good the bread is, and can we have another basket, please; they don't have moderately priced restaurants with fresh, tasty ingredients like these in Bridgeport. The marinara sauce for dipping is almost as good as her grandmother's, she admits. Italian Americans always believe their sauce is God, but I'm sure theirs is nothing like authentic Italian cuisine. I'm just as guilty as her: in my mind, my father's sauce was the best. The last time I had it I was in my adolescent years before he fell off the wagon hard and for good. Who knows what I would think of it as an adult with more refined tastes, if he were still alive and well enough to make it.

Tara has to pee and asks if I'll hold Lacy, to which I acquiesce but not without a sense of nervous apprehension. I'm still feeling woozy, my usual fear of dropping a baby amplified. Not only that, I don't know if I want her that close to me. I feel like oil: thick and greasy from decades of self-inflicted loss, failed unhealthy relationships and countless bad choices; and she's just this little lake of crystal-clear water, PH-balanced for love and an excitement for a whole life she has yet to experience. To acknowledge this creature is my niece is a terrifying responsibility for which I consider myself unqualified and perhaps undeserving.

Tara places her in my arms. Standing back, she observes the two of us with a sappy expression on her face. Softly gumming a Minnie Mouse pacifier, Lacy shutters her eyes, turns her head toward my chest, softening my anxiety. Maybe I'm okay with this.

"Oh Mickey," Tara gushes.

Looking up from his food with a smile, my brother says, "You know, if I ever die, my two beauties will always take care of you."

"Yes, we will," confirms Tara, walking toward the bathroom.

"God, Mick, stop. I'm not an invalid."

"Family's all you've got is all I'm saying. Today is proof of that." His morbid sentiment is a dead ringer for Jacques's, so it's hard to digest. Whenever I'm in trouble Mickey makes it his fault, as if he were the failed stand-in for our parents that I never asked him to be. There'd been worse incidents than last night of which he'd never caught wind. If he had, he'd have nailed himself to a cross years ago.

A gaggle of obnoxiously giddy girls pops into the restaurant, startling Lacy as the door slams behind them, her peaceful snooze shifting to an ear-piercing wail.

"Please take her."

"Okay, alright, Daddy's coming." He starts to get up, but Tara rushes back in.

"I got her, don't worry. It's okay, baby! Shhh…" In her mother's arms she quiets almost instantly.

A shrieking laugh turns my head. With penthouse cheekbones, a bone-white complexion, black-hole hair and iMessage-blue eyes, the offending chick bears a striking resemblance to Zoe Severin, Jacques's ex-girlfriend and co-star of *One Degree*. The pic on his iPhone of his cock inside her while she was having her period crosses my mind. The waiter serves me a bowl of rabbit ragù.

"Thanks."

"Enjoy," he says, heading for the girls' table to take their order, inadvertently blocking my visual of the Zoe lookalike, which is probably for the best.

TARA'S PACKING UP the baby while Mickey's shitting, the smell of it slithering under the bathroom door into the rest of the apartment. I burn one of the two Mrs. Meyer's Clean Day scented candles I bought the last day I saw Jacques—the lavender—place it on the kitchen table and use it to light a cigarette, forgetting for a second that the windows are closed and there's a baby in here. Our parents and their friends would puff and drink year round at the kitchen table, a cloud of cigar and cigarette smoke seemingly a permanent fixture in our home; and we're still alive and kicking—for the most part—so I'm partially convinced this whole smoking-is-death idea is a product of popular culture, but that's likely just my addiction talking.

"Oops, sorry, forgot about the baby," I say, putting the cigarette out on the lid of the candle.

"It's okay. You'll get around to quitting. I did after the baby, and Mickey's cut way back."

"Yeah."

"All set?" Mickey asks, emerging from the toilet.

"Jesus, Mick, your shits are deadly. I almost forgot."

"Give me a break. You know my lactose problem." He burps, pats his belly. "Too much of everything. But I think that was the best Italian restaurant I've ever been to."

"All right, relax. It's not that serious," I say.

"There's the snooty you we know and love. I can always tell you're feeling better when you start copping an attitude."

"Yeah, I'm okay."

"Promise? I'm a little worried about leaving you alone."

"Of course. You guys have to go. We all have work tomorrow."

"What about Easter Sunday?" Tara asks. "We'd be happy to come and cook dinner here."

"No, no. It's okay. I'll take the train with Max... I'm not going to Mass, though."

"Completely fine, babe. We usually go early, anyway."

"All right. Well, thanks for coming. I do appreciate you guys." Kiss cheeks goodbye. Hug bodies. Pet the dog after they depart. Lie back in bed.

I wish it were the weekend, but tomorrow's only Thursday. There'll be a great of deal of catching up to do at the office, not to mention seeing Rosemarie, which I'm not dreading as much as I would be if I weren't medicated, the same attitude applying to the Metro-North trek home: taking the train on the New Haven line, passing the Stepford stops where the boat-shoed bankers exit to their childhood homes in golden Darien, wealthy Westport and parts of Fairfield, to towns that exude a pseudo-small-town feel created by homemaking trophy moms and multi-million-dollar dads. During Easter, Metro-North is a wormhole reversing my rebirth in New York City to the unsettling familiarity of my origins in the rundown streets of Bridgeport, Connecticut; but it doesn't feel so bad to think about this time. Whether I want to admit it or not, as hard as it is to be intimate with my family, being around them is good for me right now.

Falling into a dream of nothingness—no Eyeballs, no Jacques fantasies—I'm rudely interrupted by the doorbell. Through the peephole I see a round man holding a square package. Open the door.

"Hi."

"Delivery."

"How'd you get upstairs?"

"Front door unlocked."

"I didn't order anything."

"From Cast Iron Gallery?" It's the painting I bought from that gallery in SoHo during my last day with Jacques.

"Oh yeah, sorry. I'm half asleep." He hands me the package. I rest it against the wall just inside the entrance.

"Thanks," I say, quickly signing for it.

"Have a good day."

I tear off the paper. Reveal the unmoving man on a dirty mattress, his face shrouded in a blanket, knife on the floor beside him. Jacques was wrong about this not being healthy. Hanging it over my bed, I'll be reminded of how close I came to losing my mind again.

Neighbors are laughing in the hall outside my apartment. I hear goats screaming like hysterical humans, probably playing from a video on one of their phones. Flashback to Jacques: us cackling at YouTubes of crazed goats until we couldn't breathe.

From then on, whenever I was upset with him he'd spit in my face and bleat to make me laugh, his way of apologizing—either that or sob he was sorry.

With the happy memory come others: blowing him through the fly of his tuxedo pants before he left for an awards show to which he hadn't invited me because I wasn't famous arm candy; Lake George, where we pasted temporary heart tattoos on each other's forearms, before getting lost on the drive home with dead phones and him punching my arm, wishing to God he hadn't left the shoot in Budapest to be with me; his flaunting a series of video selfies he'd made with his co-star Bree Harringway, on whom he unapologetically confessed having had a massive crush while shooting an indie romance film; exchanging thoughtful Christmas presents preceding a tragic threesome on New Year's Eve. The romantic idylls in our tumultuous relationship were always blackened by conflict, a violent clashing of neuroses for which the only cure was separation: the Death of Us. I suppose the same went for my parents, for Pedro and me and for the demons, not to mention the others I'd loved. For the first time in my life being alone is comforting: an opportunity to determine what my soul is lacking and how to resolve or accept it instead of desperately searching again for a fix in someone else.

Lying on my back in bed, I reach underneath it for my iPhone charger. When I plug it in, it doesn't work, even when jiggling the loose wire the way I usually do to get it going. Finally accepting that it's dead and that my phone will die during the night and no one will be able to reach me—even Jacques, if he calls to check up on me or changes his mind altogether—I yank it out of the wall and carry it to the trashcan in the bathroom. The stink of Lacy's diaper, mingled with the lingering stench of my brother, is almost bearable.

CHRISTOPHER STODDARD is the author of three other novels: *The Virtuous Ones* (Itna Press, 2022), *Limiters* (Itna Press, 2014), and *White, Christian* (Spuyten Duyvil, 2010). *At Night Only* was praised by PEN award-winning author Edmund White, and was a staff pick in *The Paris Review*. For more than a decade, he worked at various ad agencies in New York City. He lives in Los Angeles.